The Girl from Ipanema

William J. Gillespie

iUniverse, Inc.
Bloomington

The Girl from Ipanema

iUniverse books may be ordered through booksellers or by contacting:

iUniverse
1663 Liberty Drive
Bloomington, IN 47403
www.iuniverse.com
1-800-Authors (1-800-288-4677)

ISBN: 978-1-4697-8607-0 (sc)
ISBN: 978-1-4697-8608-7 (e)

Printed in the United States of America

iUniverse rev. date: 5/10/2012

Thanks to the following for their help and support: Patricia Gillespie, Virginia Keith, Mark and Jane Peterman, and Nancy Smith.

Cover by
Gary Smith

Chapter 1

BOOBS MONTJOY ARRIVED BY HELICOPTER at the Hooker County Courthouse dressed in a purple Versace pantsuit and a black Mongolian cashmere shrug. When the aircraft landed on the front lawn it woke up Tex Roberts, a tall, thin ninety-year-old man who was seated on a bench outside Sheriff Creel's office. The moment he saw Boobs get out of the helicopter, he was surprised to see not only the helicopter parked on the front lawn, but the way Boobs was dressed. Tex was completely taken back and thought to himself, *What the heck is going on around here? Somebody die or somethin'?*

Boobs, a strikingly handsome young woman, came barging in and yelled with great urgency, "Get out of my way, old man. I've got to see the good doctor. I need to get him to accompany me to Chicago right now!"

Old Tex Roberts was so surprised by her fancy helicopter arrival and the way she was dressed. He squinted at her and said in his Texas twang, "You're dressed as fancy as I've ever seen a woman, but there ain't no way you're ever gonna git Pee Wee on that whirlybird. He ain't been off the ground in anything since World War II. If he wasn't playing poker with that fine-lookin' sheriff, he might follow you to hell, as good as you look, 'cept it wouldn't be on no airplane or helicopter; it'd have ta be on the ground."

Boobs blushed for the first time since she'd been in grade school. She cleared her throat, swallowed, and patted Tex on the shoulder before she knocked on Sheriff Creel's door and cooed, "Damn, Tex, those are the sweetest words I've heard from a man in years, unless he was trying to get something out of me. We'll see, we'll see. Maybe when he learns the urgency of the situation, I can get him to change his mind."

"I don't think so, ma'am. He seems to be having a good time. He's done stripped that fine-lookin' sheriff down to the skin four times, and it don't look like she's gonna quit 'til she's cleaned out her closet."

"Well, we'll see, we'll see," Boobs nervously said as she proceeded to pound on the door to the sheriff's office. Then she called out for Dr. Suggs. "Open the door. Bernie's sick and you're the only doctor he'll see."

Dr. Suggs was so shocked by the pounding on the door and the loud request that he stood abruptly and almost fell as he reached over and removed a thin cotton blanket from the bed to wrap around the shivering, naked Mertis Creel before proceeding to open the door.

Boobs rushed in and mockingly said, "Damn, good doctor, I'm ashamed of you, taking advantage of this fine-looking, innocent young lady."

He blushed, sniffed, cleared his throat, and squeaked out, "My goodness, what are you talking about?"

"You, that's who!" Boobs forcefully said, trying to embarrass him in order to get him to quit playing poker and come with her.

Doc stood mute with his mouth open, staring at Boobs in her expensive designer outfit and wondering why she had said what she did. Didn't she know that it was Mertis's idea that they play strip poker? Couldn't she remember? It hadn't been that long since Mertis had gotten him to play Texas Hold 'em with her. It was true that he enjoyed cheating in Texas Hold' em, but he had no desire to do anything to Mertis except beat her at cards. Didn't she realize as a physician he had seen all the naked bodies he ever wanted to see?

Mertis had not liked Boobs since she had lived in Hooker County years ago and tried to recruit her to become an exotic dancer at the Purple Pussy Cat.

With that, Mertis reached down and got her .44 Magnum pistol with a nine-inch barrel and demanded that she and Doc be seated because the game wasn't over.

Doc and Boobs were justifiably frightened by the sight of the gun and the tone of Mertis's voice and immediately plopped down in some chairs.

Doc managed to say, with his high-pitched voice breaking up, "My goodness, Mertis—I mean Sheriff—the game is over unless you have some more clothes. Anyway, I can't stand to see you sitting there naked, shaking like that. You might come down with pneumonia."

"For your information, you old cheat," Mertis screamed out, "I'm not that damn cold, and I've still got this pair of fancy earrings, so this game ain't over yet."

"Y'all quit arguing," Boobs said as she stared at the gun. "I've got to get the good doctor to go see Bernie. He's really sick in Chicago and won't move until the good doctor examines him."

"Shut up, you overdressed hussy," Mertis ordered. "I'm gonna drill you with this gun if you don't keep quiet. Don't you know the rules of poker? Anyway, I don't care what happens to Bernard Swindle after what he did to my daddy when the furniture factory exploded. The very idea of him saying that my old man cutting the grass close to the gas main could have caused the regulator to malfunction. Everybody knows that that was in August and it didn't explode 'til February. Now either go in the other room and keep quiet, or get in the game. I could use that fancy—whatever that thing is that you've got around you shoulders."

Doc, having studied the two women closely, was no longer as scared of Mertis as he had been initially and, in a calm voice, asked her to put the gun down. When she laid her gun back on the floor, he sheepishly said, "Ladies, I guess it's put-up-or-get-out time."

Mertis didn't like the way he said it one bit. "Boobs ain't no lady, and it's put-up time, you old rogue. I ought to pistol-whip you."

Doc noticed how addled she was, smiled, and said, "Okay, dear, if you insist on playing your earrings against the pocket watch the town gave me for all my years of service."

"Don't call me dear, you old cheat," Mertis lashed out. "My earrings are worth a lot more that that six-dollar pocket watch Archibald bought at that pawnshop."

Doc knew it was a cheap watch that didn't run half the time, but he never imagined that the community would let Archibald do such a thing. A six-dollar pocket watch for forty years of service—was that all he was worth to them? A cheap watch from a pawnshop.

The ladies noticed the sad expression on his face, and Mertis teared up and said, "I'm sorry, Doc, I shouldn't have said that, but it's true. How do you think Archibald got the money to go on that missionary trip to Peru? He kept the rest of the money that the community had collected to pay for his ticket after buying that watch from old Slick Willie. When some of the men in town heard what he had done, they said if he ever came back they were going to incorporate him in the concrete foundation at the new three-hole outhouse they are planning to build at the stockyard."

Boobs was still nervous. She looked over at Mertis and asked if she could wait in the next room until the game was over.

Doc was relieved when Mertis agreed and said, "Okay, Mertis, what are the earrings worth?"

"Everything you've got on, except that old hat with the crown burned out."

"Okay, deal. I've gotta finish you off so I can find out what Miss Boobs wants with me."

"Hush," she said as she nervously dealt them two hole cards.

He ended up with a pair of treys—not a very good hand.

Mertis was ecstatic as she noticed that she had a pair of Jacks and started to jiggle her left foot, which was one of many ways Mertis gave herself away when she was playing poker.

"Okay, Mertis, let's see the flop since you haven't got anything else to bet."

Mertis had a deuce, and Doc a trey. This caused Mertis to develop a little tick in her right eyelid, which led Doc to believe that he had her and she knew it, even though the only cards showing were small in number. Mertis's turn card and the River ended up being a nine and a five.

With this, Doc turned over the two hole cards and said, "Gosh, Mertis, can you beat this?"

When she saw the three treys, she didn't bother to turn her hole cards; she just threw them at him, dropped her head down on the table, and started pounding on it and crying, "You old cheat! How did you do it? Damn you, damn you! I ought to put you in the basement with them rats. Anyway, you're not going to Chicago with that Boobs thing. We're gonna have it out."

Doc calmly replied in his squeaky voice, "Mertis, set up and let me get you some clothes out of the pile on the floor and help you put them on. We can't have a naked sheriff running around town."

The first thing he picked up was a pair of cherry-red panties with a Neiman Marcus label in them. "My goodness, Mertis," he screeched, "do you have two pairs from Neiman Marcus, or was the pair I took off of you earlier some other brand?"

Mertis lifted up her head, wiped the tears from her eyes with the blanket, and said, "Who knows."

He sniffed, cleared his throat, stuck them in his back pocket, and said, "I don't know, but I'm gonna keep these until we can find out."

She just smiled and coyly said, "You evil old man, what am I going to do with you?"

"I don't know, Mertis. I just don't know. But let's get you dressed before you shoot me or hang me or put me down in the basement again with the rats."

With that, he reached over and got a pair of flesh-colored panties and helped her put them on. "Now turn around and let me hook your bra and find you a pair of pants and a shirt that's not wrinkled."

When she was dressed, she reached over, removed his hat, kissed his bald head, and seductively said, "You old cheat. You're the first man that ever helped me dress. In spite of the fact that you cheat at cards and do all the other things that you do around town that everybody knows about, you are still a perfect gentleman."

Chapter 2

When Mertis was completely dressed and had repaired herself back to respectability, she and Doc joined Boobs in the office. Before they could say anything, Boobs reached in her bra and pulled out ten thousand-dollar bills and pleaded, "Sheriff, I've gotta make bail for him. He needs to go to Chicago right now to see Mr. Swindle. So, if you'll complete the necessary paperwork and get the judge from Fenton to set bail, I'll pay it and we can be on our way."

At first Mertis balked. Not only did she dislike Boobs and Swindle, but she didn't want to let the old man out until she had a chance to beat him at poker.

Boobs, who had been humiliated most of her life, particularly in her line of work, got down on her knees and groveled.

That did it. When Mertis noticed her groveling and saw the money on the table in front of her, she relented and said, "I'll let him out on bail if you'll promise to get him back as soon as possible. We've got to finish this poker game."

Without thinking, Doc made one of his classic verbal mistakes. "Dang, Mertis, what is it about you and this poker stuff? Are you addicted to Texas Hold 'em, or do you just like losing to me?"

This caused Mertis to angrily reply, "I ain't addicted to no poker, and I can't stand losing to you. I've just gotta find out how you go about cheatin', you old rogue. Now you and this thing get outta here before I change my mind. That is, if that's what y'all are really up to."

Boobs grabbed Doc by the arm and led him out into the hall to where Tex was still seated.

"Damn, Pee Wee, why'd you quit and give that sheriff her clothes back? Did you imagine you heard your mother calling you from the grave about how bad it was to be playing cards, or were you overcome by the desire to go with this good-looking fancy lady to Chicago?"

Boobs castigated him. "Damn, Tex, how do you know what went on between the good doctor and us? You've got it all wrong. He's not interested in me. He's going with me to see a sick patient."

Tex dropped his head and contritely said, "Ma'am, I didn't mean nothing by what I said. I was just going by what I heard through the ventilation system and the way he looks at you."

"Tex, you have a dirty mind. Don't you know better than that? The very idea of you listening in on other people's conversation. Now if you don't mind your own business I'm not going to take you back home again when it's raining, much less let you know when the next poker game takes place. One more thing, don't call him Pee Wee again."

"Yes, ma'am, if you say so. One thing for sure, you ain't gonna get him on one of them whirlybirds or in no airplane."

"Whatta you mean?"

"Just what I said to you earlier, young lady. He ain't been off the ground since he got shot down the last time in China and almost lost his right leg."

With that, Tex looked out the front door at the helicopter parked on the front lawn, squinted, and said, "Yep, there ain't no way. He ain't been in no plane since he got shot down over yonder."

Doc stood there frozen, thinking about how afraid he had been, flying the Burma Hump until the Japanese retreated.

Boobs looked down at the frightened old man and asked if what Tex had said was true.

Doc barely mumbled, his voice breaking up. "Yes, ma'am, I'm afraid so."

This led her to wonder what she would do now. It would take fifteen hours by car.

While she was contemplating the next move, old Tex spoke up. "You can drive him into town and get 'em to catch the City of New Orleans. He ain't a'feared of riding on no train. It's a shame what happened to him during the war. Yep, I imagine his wife he met overseas took everything away from him, except for these women he's sleeping with around here." This caused Doc to become so weak he had to sit down. *Does everyone know how passive I've been all my life?*

Old Tex shook his head and continued. "My, how he loves to sleep around with the women."

This caused the poor doctor to sniff and cough and feel as bad he did the time his mother got on him when she caught him looking at the lady's underwear section in the Sears Roebuck catalog.

Boobs got on Tex again for talking the way he did about Doc, placed her arm around Dr. Suggs, and softly said, "Honey, don't pay any attention to Tex. You aren't afraid. When Bernie and I checked up on you we found out that you had earned two Distinguished Flying Crosses and a whole host of other medals. You are a real war hero. They don't pass those things out to just anybody. To hell with flying; we'll see how fast we can get there in Bernie's gas-guzzling Bentley. That is, if you drive it like you did that souped-up whiskey car you got from Skeeter when you shot up that methamphetamine lab when you were investigating those nursing home deaths." Boobs then called for the car and sent the helicopter back to the airport.

Chapter 3

Doc wasn't too happy about driving any car, much less a Bentley. In fact, he had rarely driven over fifty or a hundred miles at a time except when he took his father to Panama City to get him out of town while he was investigating the nursing home deaths. He needed some of the courage he had long since lost. The next best thing he could think of was a cup of coffee, and he asked Tex if he had any coffee left. Tex didn't, so he turned and went into the sheriff's office and asked, "Mertis, can I have a small cup of your delicious coffee?"

She smiled at him and said, "You damn old cheat. Why should I give you a cup of coffee after the way you left the poker game for a stripper to check on that no-account lawyer—that is, if that's where y'all are going? I think I just might tell all your lady friends around here how you left here with Boobs all dolled up the way she is and let them draw their own conclusions."

The uneasy old man blurted out, "My goodness, Mertis, don't you understand? I'm a doctor and I can't refuse to see a patient. Didn't you notice the way Miss Boobs was down on her knees begging you? Mr. Swindle must be very ill. Now how about a cup of coffee so I can go and do what I've got to do? The sooner I go, the sooner I'll be back to finish the game. That is, if you've got any clothes left other than the ones that I've loaned you."

Mertis just smiled and in a soft voice said, "Well, it's going to be interesting to see what you do with that stripper. I wonder if the good ladies in Hooker County will believe that you really drove all the way to Chicago, as scared as you are of driving out of town, to look after that no-account, bloodsucking lawyer. There are more doctors in the city of Chicago than there are in this whole state."

Chapter 4

Doc surprised himself and scared Boobs to death on the drive to Chicago. He drove as fast as it would go, only stopping to get gasoline and slowing down when he passed through Memphis and St. Louis. It was as if he were back flying again, feeling free as a bird and making rice drops over Burma. He was away from home with no one to tell him what to do and what not to do—just to fly anywhere except over the Burma Hump. All in all the drive was a joyful experience for him, but not to Boobs because she remained frightened the whole time.

There he was, a young man again flying a C-47, outfoxing the Japanese—that is, before his last crash, which ended him in the hospital and marrying his now-deceased wife.

When they arrived at the hotel where Swindle was staying, Boobs had a heated argument with the parking garage attendant since the hotel was full and they didn't have reservations. Finally, they overcame this little obstacle when Boobs reached in her bra and pulled out fifty dollars.

Doc was amazed. He had always known that money made a lot of things happen, but the way Boobs and Swindle used it made it seem like it could make anything happen. It was almost as if money had some magical power.

The whole trip had been like a dream. He could hardly believe what he had done and that they were now in Chicago waiting to go and check on Bernard Swindle.

When they finally got up to Swindle's elaborate suite on the seventh floor, they found the portly, ashen attorney stretched out on the bed in his purple outfit with his large silk handkerchief stuffed in his collar like a bib.

Boobs knew what he had been up to when she saw the handkerchief stuffed in his collar. He certainly hadn't ordered ordinary room service. Without even asking first how he was feeling, she simply asked, "What happened?" Her tone of voice did not elicit any sympathy.

Swindle started thrashing about aimlessly in bed and pulled the covers over his face. He knew what Boobs was thinking.

Yes, he thought. *I couldn't resist the temptation. Should I admit it or play dumb?* Swindle decided to completely overlook her asking what had happened because he was feeling bad in addition to being frightened. With his boisterous voice breaking up, he replied, "Where in the hell have you guys been? That Latin firecracker that someone sent to entertain me just about killed me."

Dr. Suggs, who earlier had felt free and easy for the first time in over fifty years, was appalled at the way Swindle was behaving, thrashing about in the bed in his purple silk shirt with a large white handkerchief stuffed in his collar. It reminded him of a frightened three-year-old who was just awakening from a night terror.

Boobs knew that Swindle had been caught in one of his compulsive situations and wanted an explanation. "Bernie, just quit the whining and tell us exactly what happened."

Swindle turned over on his stomach, with his face buried in the pillow, and whined. "Do I have to give you a detailed description?"

"Yes, you big baby," Boobs angrily answered as she hit him as hard as she could on his bottom. "I'm not sure I want to know, but if the good doctor is going to help you, he may need to know."

When he didn't speak up right away, she reached under the cover and grabbed him, causing him to immediately turn on his side, facing Dr. Suggs, and start to talk. "This fine-looking young Latin firecracker approached me during the afternoon coffee break and told me that she was alone in Chicago and asked me if I would show her around."

Dr. Suggs knew what the answer was but asked anyway. "What did you think when she asked you?"

Boobs turned to Dr. Suggs. "He didn't think!"

Still short of breath and shaking all over, Swindle meekly said, "I invited her up to my suite. What was I to do? Leave this lonely foreign lady by herself in Chicago? Anyway, I've never been with a girl like her before. Certainly not one of those Latin firecrackers that look a little Chinese"

Dr. Suggs gave Boobs a perplexed look and said, "Mr. Swindle, I thought you said she was a Spanish or Latin firecracker. Wasn't that what you said?"

Swindle became addled and finally bellowed out in his lawyerly voice, "She talked and acted like a South American, but she looked like one of them good-looking, tall Chinese women."

"What was her name, and what was she doing at the meeting? Didn't you read her name tag, and exactly what kind of accent did she have? You're getting me all confused, Mr. Swindle. Was she or was she not Chinese in origin, and what happened after she got to your room? Did you get sick from some of the food you had eaten or what, since you've got your handkerchief stuffed in your collar like a bib?"

Swindle hesitated and, when he didn't speak up right away, Boobs slapped him and shouted, "Dammit, Bernie, speak up and cut out the runaround you're giving us."

He whined, "Why'd you do that, baby?"

"Because you needed it," Boobs angrily replied.

He meekly commented, "I took off my coat and got into bed while she went to the bathroom."

"That sounds just like you, Bernie," Boobs disgustedly replied.

Dr. Suggs started sniffing, snorting, clearing his throat, and thinking, *Surely he didn't do what I'm thinking with a complete stranger.*

"What happened next, Mr. Swindle?" Dr. Suggs screeched out.

"When she came out of the bathroom, she was naked and gently placed her clothes on the chair and climbed in the bed with me. Before I could get started good, she scratched me on my left shoulder and laughed. This frightened me, and I started to breathe rapidly and my lips and tongue became numb. Before I passed out, she got up and put her clothes on and started singing the lyrics to 'The Girl from Ipanema.'"

This made Dr. Suggs angry, so he got up and went to the bathroom before he lost his temper and said something he might regret. Boobs followed him to make sure he was all right.

Doc swished some water around in his mouth. Breathless, he said, "I'm not up to date on some of these contemporary things. I'm nothing but a country bumpkin." Meanwhile, he was thinking, *My goodness, this is at least the third time I've caught Bernie doing such a thing with strangers.*

Boobs angrily said, "That's Bernie's fatal compulsion. You know, he's not much of a man and does it with complete strangers."

Dr. Suggs saw a small amount of fecal matter on the rim of the toilet bowl, went to the lavatory, and got a glass to put a specimen in.

Boobs asked, "Why did you get that glass and straw?"

He squeaked, "The commode has fecal matter in it. Go ask Mr. Swindle who used it last."

This made absolutely no sense to Boobs, so she asked, "Why?"

"Because I need to know whose fecal matter is in there."

"What will that prove, good doctor?"

"If it's not Mr. Swindle's, maybe it will tell us something about the young, Chinese-looking, Latin lady's dietary habits."

Boobs shouted, "Bernie, who used the toilet last?"

"Why?"

"Because the good doctor wants to know, that's why."

"That Chinese-looking Latin firecracker, the one who sang 'The Girl from Ipanema' while she thought I was dying."

Chapter 5

Boobs rejoined Swindle in the bedroom, where he was still thrashing around aimlessly and crying, "What in the hell is that old man still doing in the bathroom? Can't he see that I might be dying from what that pig did to me? Can't he see that she stuck me with some poison in my left shoulder?"

Boobs was still angry about his behavior and at the same time frightened over the possibility that he might be seriously ill. She bluntly replied, "He's collecting a stool specimen."

Swindle bounced up on the side of the bed and bellowed out, "What? That old fart's in there playing in the toilet when he should be out here examining me?"

This infuriated Boobs, and she slapped him so hard that you could hear it out in the hall and lashed out, "Damn, you worthless bastard, don't call him an old fart. He's not going to let you die. I don't know why he's doing what he's doing, but I'm sure he has a good reason."

When Swindle started to cry again, she got up on the side of the bed and hugged him. "Now, big baby, don't cry around the good doctor. You've got to protect your image. When we get home, I'll give you a good spanking for doing what you did with that Latin girl. You know you're not supposed to have anything to do with a woman unless I approve of her. You could ruin your reputation and all we've worked for. Now try to relax and let the good doctor take care of things. I thought after the affair with old man Bigelow's wife, you were going to let me check out your women for you. I've saved you from yourself over the years and made you what you are today, and don't you ever forget."

After Boobs finished chastising Swindle, he calmed down and meekly said, "I'm sorry, baby. I guess I do need a good spanking."

When Dr. Suggs finished collecting the stool specimen and placed it in one of the sealed drinking glasses next to the lavatory, he walked back into the room where they were and asked if they had heard a noise that sounded like a slap.

Boobs quickly replied, "Yes. It must have come from the room next door."

Dr. Suggs couldn't help but notice Swindle's red cheek and didn't believe her for one minute. He dropped it at that and asked her if she would fetch his medical bag for him.

Dr. Suggs meticulously opened it with his small hands and removed a scalpel and a hemostat and assiduously removed a large piece of his silk shirt from the area where the so-called girl from Ipanema had allegedly injected something into his shoulder. Underneath his clothing was nothing but a small superficial scratch mark.

"Hmm," Dr. Suggs said. "I don't know whether we have anything here or not, but we'll see. Miss Boobs, would you fetch me another glass from the bathroom?"

Boobs wasn't sure why he wanted it but did as he instructed. He then proceeded to do a complete physical and neurological examination and swab his mouth and face for evidence of drugs and DNA.

Doc then proceeded to stare up at the ceiling and run through all the various things that she could have used in an effort to poison him. He immediately ruled out ricin because of the lapse of time between the call and the time they arrived. He would have loved to have taken a biopsy on the scratch mark without using anesthesia, but he knew that Swindle couldn't tolerate the pain. He thought, *I might as well forget it. This big blowhard can't stand pain. Maybe something will turn up from what I've removed, since it does seem the only place damp with something that could have poison on it.*

Dr. Suggs then asked, "Mr. Swindle, what do you think she stuck you with?"

"I'm not sure, because I had my eyes closed," he moaned. "The only thing I remember was she had a large ring on her right hand."

Boobs continued to wonder what was going on in Dr. Suggs's mind but didn't ask. She felt that if he had any concern about needing anyone else to see

Mr. Swindle, he would refer him on like he did the time when he connected the pulmonary infection with smoking marijuana contaminated with dung.

Her train of thought was interrupted by Swindle nervously asking, "I'm not going to die, am I, good doctor?"

Doc wasn't sure but squeaked out in his high-pitched voice, "No, sir. Looks like you're going to be lucky—at least that's the way it seems so far." He proceeded to draw three tubes of blood to send to the lab and gave him a cup to collect a urine specimen.

When Doc's words finally soaked in, Swindle tried to sit up in bed, but Boobs restrained him.

"Damn, whatta you mean, 'so far'?"

"I mean, for one thing, whoever's after you, Mr. Swindle, is probably still here at the meeting or close by and will remain here until they are sure you are dead. Now would you please calm down and let me think."

Dr. Suggs paced around the room with his hands behind his back, mumbling incoherently and thinking about how he could go about identifying and locating the woman in question, who Swindle called the girl from Ipanema. This was a fancy hotel; surely they had cameras everywhere, including in the elevators.

Boobs didn't want to upset the attorney any more than necessary, but she had to ask. "Damn, Bernie, everything's been so crazy that I forgot to ask if you recorded the session with her like you usually do behind my back. You know, like when the nurse from Southwest Hospital stops by to give you information about what's going on at the HMO."

Swindle cowered, pulled the cover up over his face, and sheepishly said, "Yes, ma'am, it's under the bed, but I didn't film it." Afraid he might be slapped again, he continued to hold the covers up around his face.

"Fool!" she shouted. "When will you ever learn? What if one of these recordings ever gets in the wrong hands?"

Swindle was still whining. "I'm sorry, baby, the only reason I did it was if anything ever turned up, I could prove that it was consensual. You know how it is with women when they're dealing with someone as prominent as I am."

Dr. Suggs turned red and then pale and finally ended up becoming angry. *Does this fella really think he's that important? My goodness, he has more than one fatal flaw. He can't do it like a man and is so perverted he even records it.*

Boobs gave Swindle a look like she wanted to kill him. She then got down on the floor and retrieved the tape recorder and purple thong from under the bed. When she arose she turned to Dr. Suggs and asked, "Good doctor, do you think you have the stomach to listen to this?" Boobs held up the purple thong and asked, "Bernie, is this hers?"

"I guess so, but she didn't have it on when she came in here from the bathroom."

Doc looked moribund, felt his heart rate soar, and thought, *My goodness, all this time I thought Boobs was the kinky one. She's the brains, the gatekeeper, so to speak. She has this poor fella scared out of his wits. I guess I would be too if one of the ladies at home slapped me when I was down and out.*

When they started to play the tape, Boobs stopped it briefly. She looked at Doc and tried to make an excuse for Swindle. "I guess he's been scared out of his wits since old man Bigelow chased him out of town and tried to kill him when he caught him with his wife."

Dr. Suggs wondered what the heck this had to do with the tape. It was quite obvious to him that Swindle was afraid of Boobs, which made him think, *Am I as afraid of my mother as Swindle is of Boobs? If I am, I don't have any reason to be, but he sure does.*

The dialogue between the girl and Swindle was so raunchy that Dr. Suggs could barely remain still and listen to it. When they got to the part where Swindle had mentioned that she had a fine-looking caramel heart, Dr. Suggs turned pale, got up, stumbled into the bathroom, and cursed out loud. Hearing something like that was a problem for Dr. Suggs. It's true he was from a different generation, but the way they talked made him feel like he could no longer tolerate the thought of it. He wondered, *Are very many men like him? I know some of the younger ones do these sorts of things every now and then, but my goodness, what's the world coming to, particularly if this is the only way this man can do it? Hasn't he heard of the germ theory?* Here was this woman he had never seen or heard of before, and he took her up to his room and did what he did.

Boobs stopped the tape, followed Doc into the bathroom, and attempted to apologize for Swindle. "You gonna be all right, good doctor? I'm sorry you had to see this side of Bernie. Oh, how I wish he were more like you. Are you sure you're gonna be all right?"

Dr. Suggs squeaked out, "I think so, but I don't believe I can listen to any more of that tape. It's not that I'm all that good; it's just that I never thought Mr. Swindle was into something like that so deep. I guess I'm just dated. Anyway, after listening to what I've heard, I'm glad that my time's about up."

When Dr. Suggs had recovered sufficiently from listening to as much of the tape as he could, he returned to the room, took a seat next to the bed, and told Boobs and Mr. Swindle what he thought they needed to do next.

"Number one," Dr. Suggs said more forcefully than he had spoken before, "I can't tell you where the woman is from—that is, if she was really trying to kill you. I don't know anything about linguistics, but there is nothing in her speech pattern to suggest that she's Chinese. You know, I still remember a good bit of Chinese, and it doesn't sound like she's from any province I'm familiar with. It sounds more like a mixture of Spanish and some Latin American Indian dialect, mixed in with English. But we need to get someone who's an expert, like for instance, hire some graduate student from the University of Chicago to give us an idea about the dialect."

When he said that, Swindle sprung up in the bed and bellowed out in his lawyerly voice, "Damn, I can't do that. I've got too much to lose."

"The hell you can't," Boobs shouted. "You mean you'd rather run the risk that this person may try to kill you again."

Dr. Suggs interrupted. "What was that last thing she said when she left the room?"

Boobs asked him if he wanted her to play the rest of the tape, and he said, "No, no, please don't. Just tell me what you think."

"I think she said, 'Now dream of Jeanie with the light-brown hair. Bye-bye.'"

"Hmm," Dr. Suggs said. "There are not very many female serial killers. However, her actions and the way she seemed to know a good bit about you and what you enjoy lead me to believe she's made contact with someone from your past. Counselor, do you know a Jeanie with light-brown hair?"

Swindle had a surprised look on his face, but he didn't say anything.

Boobs thought, *"Jeanie with light-brown hair. Bye-bye." Hmm, my goodness, he's been with so many women with light-brown hair it's hard to say if what she said really meant anything.*

Dr. Suggs spoke up again. "Heck, let's leave it there, and y'all think about it. Now, we must find out where this so-called girl from Ipanema is."

Doc got up again and started walking around the room, mumbling to himself. "Aha, that's it!"

Boobs and Swindle became very attentive and stared at him.

"Yep, that's it, folks. We need to check with security and see if we can find her on the cameras. What time would you say she stopped by to see you, counselor?"

Bernie whined, "Three o'clock in the afternoon."

Dr. Suggs said, "Three o'clock. I wonder how long they keep the tapes before they erase them. We must check this out. We need some money."

This statement about money surprised Boobs and Swindle. It was the first time they had ever heard Dr. Suggs mention money. In fact, all he had ever done was work hard trying to earn enough money to keep his now-deceased wife and her two greedy daughters satisfied and avoid bankruptcy with assistance from his father.

"Yep, that's it," he squeaked. "How much money do the two of you have between you?"

Boobs reached in her bra and pulled out twenty thousand dollars and another thousand from her purse. Bernie had about a thousand on him.

Dr. Suggs figured that would not be enough and asked if there was any way they could get additional money there in the next several hours. "We're going to need a lot of money."

Bernie sat up and barked out, "What in the hell do you know about money? You've never made enough to do anything with it, and what about me? You're not going to let me die, are you?"

Dr. Suggs ignored his cutting comment. "No, you're not going to die, counselor. You're perfectly stable, but I'll need the money—or, should I say, we'll need the money to carry out the scheme I have in mind. It's rather complicated—that is, if we can find out what we're looking for on the security tapes. To quote you, counselor, 'An envelope full of money is better than a whore in the bed when it comes to getting things done.'"

They were both shocked to hear Dr. Suggs use the word *whore.* He was shocked himself, to some extent, but he was still agitated about the mere thought of what Bernie had done.

"Hurry up and make up your mind, counselor. Are you gonna get the money here? Because what we are going to do next is going to be critical. We don't want anyone stalking you for the remainder of your days. We want to end this right here and now, if at all possible."

Swindle fumed and hesitated a few seconds but finally told Boobs to tell Jessica to get the tan alligator briefcase out of his personal safe and have Big Boy Jones bring it to Chicago on his private jet.

With that, Dr. Suggs said, "Good," and went to the phone and called his old army friend, General Higgins, to get Roscoe Turner's number.

"General, I need Roscoe Turner's phone number, but first tell me how you, Frances, and the children are. No, I'm not in trouble. I need to check with him about something unrelated to me."

He wrote down the number and said, "Give Frances my love, and I hope to see you both soon," and placed down the receiver.

Chapter 6

Dr. Suggs got permission from Swindle to take a shower and shave. By the time he had finished, Boobs had pressed his coat, had the door rekeyed to Swindle's suite, and they immediately went to security.

The hotel security section was locked, and after knocking on the door for quite some time, a middle-aged woman, with her hair and makeup in total disarray, answered the door. She sharply asked, "What's the nature of your visit?" It was obvious that Mrs. Collette DeLors was not expecting visitors.

Dr. Suggs stated softly in his high-pitched voice, "Ma'am, we just need to get you to check a little information for us, that's all."

"I'm not sure we can do that," Collette replied. "Me and Henry are in charge of monitoring everything that goes on in the hotel, and strangers are not allowed inside. And anyway, we can't give out information to strangers."

Boobs pulled out a thousand dollars and softly said, "All we're trying to do is locate someone. Here, we'll make it worth your time."

When Collette DeLors saw the money, she turned to Henry and said, "I think it will be all right if we let these people come in. What do you think, Henry?"

Henry was a frightened young man, who appeared to be young enough to be her son. He finally spoke. "You're the boss. Whatever you think, but maybe they should come back at another time, if you know what I mean."

Dr. Suggs was quick to say, "Folks, I would like to, but it's really imperative that we locate this particular lady immediately, and as my associate said, we will certainly make it worth your while."

When Henry saw the thousand dollars and the excited look on Collette's face, he agreed.

"If my memory serves me correctly, madam, the lady in question met this attorney during a coffee break at the trial lawyers' convention yesterday. It is madam, isn't it?" Dr. Suggs asked.

"Yes. Why?"

"Oh, I just wanted to be correct. As best I can tell, she left there with this attorney."

Henry looked at Boobs and Dr. Suggs and asked, "You're not up to anything illegal, are you?"

Boobs smiled at Henry and quickly replied, "Absolutely not."

With that, Dr. Suggs took out a hundred dollar bill, placed it on the counter between them, and asked, "Would you mind looking at your tape to see what happened at three o'clock yesterday outside of the conference room?"

At first they balked, but Boobs smiled at them and said, "We're not interested in what y'all were doing before we came in, and we're certainly not going to inform anyone else as to what you guys have been doing, because what goes on behind closed doors is absolutely none of our business. Isn't that right, boss?"

Dr. Suggs answered, "Absolutely. My only suggestion to y'all would be that maybe Collette should not wear makeup at times like this, if y'all can't restrain yourselves until you get off work."

Collette seemed addled. Henry was so frightened he was shaking.

"What do you mean?" Collette asked in a distressed tone of voice.

"You know what he meant. Surely, you don't think we're fools, do you?" Boobs replied.

"Oh, whatta you mean?" Henry asked.

The prudish Dr. Suggs tried to smile. "Young man, it is readily apparent that she didn't get this disheveled and get her makeup smeared all over you while you were monitoring what was going on in the hotel. Here, take another fifty dollars and think about it."

When he placed the fifty dollars on the counter between them, they both seemed to drop all objections to doing what was requested.

"That's good," Dr. Suggs curtly said. "Let's proceed with what we need to do. All we're interested in is finding this particular lady. We're not interested in the attorney, but we really must locate her, and when we do, all we're gonna do is have a little talk with her. It's just that simple."

Henry and Collette looked at each other, and she finally spoke up. "Henry, dear, we have nothing to lose and quite a bit to gain if they're telling us the truth. I believe them when they say they're not going to tell on us."

Henry, who was still frightened, said with his voice cracking, "Yes, dear."

Dr. Suggs placed another fifty dollars on the counter between them and said, "Here, you can buy a pretty good bottle of champagne the next time you're able to be together away from work."

Mrs. DeLors, or Collette, grabbed the money.

Dr. Suggs pointed out to them that it was for both of them. Collette grabbed Henry's hand, placed the money in it, squeezed it, and said, "Here, surprise me."

Dr. Suggs congratulated them on making the right decision, as he saw it, and said, "Now, let's proceed to see if we can't locate the woman in question."

When they reviewed the tape from the area in question outside the conference room, they saw Bernie and a good-looking South American Indian woman in her early thirties talking. A short time later, they left the coffee area together and headed for the elevator. Dr. Suggs then instructed them to zero in on the elevator. They did. He noticed that they went up to the seventh floor, got off, and went to Bernie's suite. Dr. Suggs asked them to stop the tape and make him a copy. He had a friend who could probably identify her.

They looked puzzled and somewhat frightened regarding his motives.

Boobs and Doc picked up on this and told them not to worry, that all they wanted to do was find out who she was and have a little talk with her about a very personal matter.

"Don't you remember what we said earlier?" Boobs forcefully asked.

This seemed to relieve them to some extent, particularly when Boobs placed another hundred dollars down on the counter between them and asked, "How long you guys been going together?"

Collette surprised them by answering, "Six months. Isn't that right, Henry?"

"Yes, dear. It will be six months this coming Saturday."

"Good," Boobs said. "You know, it would be nice if the two of y'all could get off and maybe go to Paris and celebrate your six-month anniversary. You will certainly have enough money by the time we're through to pay for the trip. That is, if you don't stay at a place like the Ritz."

Collette smiled, and Henry hesitantly said, "If we can get off and Marcel won't find out about it, it's certainly something to consider."

Collette reached over, squeezed his hand, and seductively said, "Yes, Henry, I think we should make plans. I can get someone to come in and cover for me, and you can take sick leave. How does that sound?"

Henry reluctantly agreed.

"Good," Doc said. "Now if I can get a picture of the young lady, I'll need to make a call and use your computer briefly."

Henry, still unsettled about the whole situation, said, "I thought you said that all you wanted to do was locate this woman so you could talk to her."

"You're absolutely right, Henry," Dr. Suggs replied in his high-pitched voice. "But in order to locate her, we need to know who she is and what room she's staying in. Doesn't that make sense to you?"

Collette wanted the money so bad that she didn't question anything and started flittering about. "I'll have them ready for you momentarily. Then what else would you have us do?"

"Only two more things," Doc said. "But first I must make a phone call."

With that, he called Turner, who immediately answered the phone. "I've been waiting on your call. What took you so long?" Turner sarcastically asked.

"We had to get a few things sorted out first. Now get on your computer. I want to download a picture for you of this particular woman at the trial lawyers' meeting in Chicago. She ran into an acquaintance of mine. I need to know who she is and where she's from. I think she's from South America somewhere, but I don't know her name or what group she's a member of. All I know is that she's here and she had an encounter with this attorney, which didn't turn out too well for him."

Turner gave Doc his password and said, "Send," and hung up.

Doc sent him the photographs. It wasn't long after that he received a reply. Her name was Marta Roho, a member of the Shining Path, which was presently located in Brazil. It seems that originally the group had been in Ayacucho, Peru, and she had been running with a fellow named Carlos Chavez, a well-known Maoist. She was originally from the United States and met Carlos in graduate school in California. They were wanted for robbing a bank in Fresno, California, five years ago. They had been recently chased out of Peru by the government and were now hiding out in Brazil.

Turner sent him fifty pages that covered her life from beginning to her current address in the south of France.

When Dr. Suggs saw this, his heart started to race, he became nauseated, and he experienced tightness in his chest. He couldn't help but wonder, *Why did I call Roscoe? I needed help in order to help Swindle, but why did I call Roscoe? I should have known that he loved to blow up places. This will make me no better than him, if he does carry out a raid on their camp.*

Chapter 7

Dr. Suggs was so disturbed by Turner saying he might bomb the Maoist camp, he forgot to ask him about some other things he would need.

He picked up the phone, dialed him again, thanked him for the information on Miss Roho, and said, "Gosh, Mr. Turner, I forgot to ask you what this Carlos fellow looks like. The plan I've got in mind for Miss Roho will require several actors from one of the local theaters in Chicago, and I'll have to know what Carlos looks like when I get someone to meet Miss Roho, in case we find her."

Roscoe laughed. "Don't worry about the actors, Dr. Suggs. I'll send five or six of my former agents by the hotel to check with you. Exactly what do you need?"

Dr. Suggs felt like his heart had leaped up into his throat, and he finally mumbled, "I need an Arabic-speaking male dressed in traditional American clothes, a couple of Hispanics, and an Arab woman. Maybe a huge black guy, if at all possible, and a makeup artist, because I want the woman dressed in a classic Arabic woman's outfit that smells like burned camel dung and goats. The Latins need to be dressed like Chicago Hispanic gang members. I really don't know about the black man. I'll just have to give it some thought. Anyway, what I'm gonna do is discuss a script with them to frighten Miss Roho out of her wits when we find her. Hopefully, she'll be more than happy to tell us who sent her here and why."

"Who sent her there? Whatta you mean, Doc?"

"My goodness, I forgot to tell you. She tried to assassinate the attorney she was with, and now that I know she's a former member of the Shining

Path, I need to shake her up in order to get her to divulge who ordered the contract."

Roscoe laughed again, making it obvious to Doc that he was enjoying the thought of doing something sadistic to Roho and maybe the other members of her group.

"Doc, from now on your name will be Percy Gibbs. I'll have those people over there in five minutes. Say you need to have a female dressed in something that smells like burned camel dung and goats?"

Doc was so upset he repeated himself, "Yes, sir; yes, sir; and the others, except the Hispanic men need to be dressed like members of a street gang and wearing perfume or whatever you want to call it, body lotion, like the Hispanics do. The Arab man—doesn't really matter whether he's got a beard or not, just as long as he's got a good Arabic accent."

"Okay, it's done, so calm down," Turner said and slammed down the phone.

Doc had forgotten one thing. He hadn't located Roho yet, and he immediately returned to where Henry and Mrs. DeLors were and told them that he needed to see if he could locate her.

They told him that they weren't sure. He put another hundred dollars on the counter between them and said, "Maybe this will help you make up your minds."

Collette's mind was made up immediately, and she seductively said, "We will, won't we, honey?"

"I guess, if you say so, dear," Henry reluctantly answered.

"I say so, and we're going to Paris." Collette hugged the nervous Henry and quivered excitedly.

Boobs chuckled and said, "You're damn right. The way you're going, you're going to be able to have a short stay at the Ritz, but I would suggest that you stay at one of the less expensive hotels like we suggested earlier and enjoy yourselves."

Mrs. DeLors smiled and started switching the cameras back and forth until she finally located Roho in the main hotel restaurant, eating a spinach salad and drinking a glass of white wine.

Dr. Suggs said, "Hmm, not a very good Communist. Look, she's got a champagne appetite. Her parents must have spoiled her before she decided to become a pseudo-Maoist or whatever she is."

Doc pointed her out to Collette and told her to go downstairs, page Roho to meet her at the elevator, and tell her that Carlos wanted her to wait for him in his room until he got to town.

Collette was reluctant and said she wasn't sure she would be able to leave the office that long.

Dr. Suggs placed another hundred dollar bill on the counter and said, "Goodness, this will give you another half a day in Paris, if you're frugal. I'm not sure you'll be going there to eat, will you, Collette?"

She smiled as she grabbed Henry on the midthigh and said, "Not unless we have to."

Henry flinched and asked what he would do if she got a call while she was away from her desk.

Boobs noticed their reluctance and pulled off her Mongolian cashmere shrug and placed it around Collette's shoulders. "I'm sure this, and my sunglasses, will disguise you from our lady. Henry can tell anyone who calls that you are in the restroom."

"Now before you go," Doc said, "my associate and I need to go downstairs and rent another room in Carlos's name and give the desk clerk a description of him."

Doc's thinking was that if she had any sense at all, she would certainly check with the desk clerk to see who was in the room. Collette told her where Carlos would be when he arrived.

"OK, folks, we'll be ready as soon as my associate and I get back," Doc said.

They left Henry and Collette and went down to one of the shops on the main floor and bought two pieces of luggage. Boobs bought a change of underwear, and Doc a sport coat to take the place of his cheap rumpled jacket.

When they arrived at the front desk to rent a room, they were quick to tell the young lady at the desk that they wanted a room where they wouldn't be disturbed for the next twelve hours.

The young lady looked at them suspiciously. However, when Boobs placed a hundred dollars in front of her, her demeanor changed. "What else can I do for you?" she quickly asked. "You know all the rooms are supposed to be full."

Dr. Suggs explained that there was a young lady who was going to meet a fellow named Carlos in room 1059, where an old man and a young woman were checking out early. "I'm sure that can be arranged," he said as he handed her a hundred dollars and a picture of Carlos.

Dr. Suggs thought it would be best to explain to her that they planned to surprise them. Boobs interceded, gave her another hundred dollars, and said, "Dear, this is going to be somewhat of a birthday special for them, and I'd prefer—and I know you would also if you were in a similar situation—that no one else knew about it. Right?"

"Oh yes, ma'am. Yes, ma'am," the clerk said, knowing that they were probably lying.

"Good. Now keep this picture, because she'll come up and check to see whether or not Carlos is really here. You know, we don't want her to be suspicious of anything. We want this to be a surprise. All you need to do is tell her whether he has arrived or not."

Dr. Suggs and Boobs returned to the security section, feeling relieved that this part of the plan had been implemented.

"Okay, but the room is rented out to a couple in the a.m.," the desk clerk said.

Chapter 8

Arriving back at security, Doc and Boobs told Henry and Collette that they were ready for the next move.

Henry anxiously asked, "What?"

Boobs smiled at him and said, "My goodness, Henry, don't you remember? Collette goes down to the lobby, has our female friend paged to meet her at the elevator, and tells her Carlos wants her to meet him in room 1059."

"Oh, oh, yes, yes."

It was obvious to them that Henry, in addition to being frightened, was not as much in love with Collette as she seemed to be with him, but they didn't dwell on it. Their affair was of no great concern to them, unless it interfered with their plans.

The Mongolian cashmere shrug made Collette feel very important, and after receiving another fifty dollars, Boobs placed her dark sunglasses on Collette, gave her a key to room 1059, and went downstairs to page Roho to meet her at the elevator.

Roho responded to the page, and the minute she reached the elevator, Dr. Suggs asked Henry to turn off the camera so that she and Collette would not be seen together.

Henry reluctantly did it.

When Collette returned to the security section, Doc and Boobs told Collette and Henry to take a break. They would watch the monitors to look for a huge man with a tan alligator briefcase and five or six other people.

Collette grabbed Henry none too gently and led him into the break room.

When Big Boy Jones arrived, Boobs went downstairs and purchased three roast beef sandwiches and a half gallon of ice cream as a reward for being so prompt and led him up to Swindle's suite.

When Dr. Suggs saw the five people he thought Turner had sent, he couldn't help but wonder where the Arab woman was. He went out in the hall, next to the elevator, and used the phone to tell the young lady they had talked to earlier at the front desk to please ask the Arabic gentleman in the black suit to come to the phone.

When Muhammed answered the phone, Dr. Suggs told him to come to Bernard Swindle's suite because they needed to have a little rehearsal before the main event.

By now Dr. Suggs was extremely nervous about the whole situation and went to the restroom in the security break room. The first thing he noticed was Collette vigorously making love to Henry. She was wearing nothing except the cashmere shrug. Seeing her pendulous breasts dangling down like pears reminded him of the time years ago when he had caught his wife in their bed with a young college student, and he immediately turned pale and started to hyperventilate.

He thought, *My goodness, what in the world is going on here? Are we all crazy? Here's this woman old enough to be this lad's mother with him pinned down on the couch, going at it and completely unconcerned about me walking into the room.* He forgot about having to use the restroom, returned to the desk where the surveillance cameras were, and took a seat next to Boobs, who had just returned from taking Big Boy Jones to Swindle's suite.

She noticed how pale and addled he was and asked, "What's happened to you? You are as white as a sheet and shaking all over."

With his voice breaking up, he quickly told her that he was in the wrong place at the wrong time. To him, this whole interlude from the time he left Mertis Creel's office until now had been one awful experience.

Boobs again asked him what was wrong, and he pointed toward the door to the break room and said, "Go see for yourself. I'm afraid I can't tell you."

Boobs quietly opened the door to the break room, peeked in, and saw Collette making love to Henry.

She smiled, closed the door, returned to where Doc was sitting, placed her arm around his shoulder, and said, "I'm sorry that you had to witness this, particularly after what Bernie's done, but at least we're getting everything set up to do whatever it is you plan to do. Do you want to leave those two lovebirds a tip before we go to Bernie's room and join the group?"

Dr. Suggs squeaked out angrily, "My goodness. Oh heck, why not. Anyway, we'll have to settle with them before we leave, or at least before Miss Roho leaves. That is, if they have decided to leave poor Marcel working in the shoe store and go to Paris for a long weekend."

"Okay, sounds good to me, but when are you going to tell me just exactly what you have in mind, you tricky old man?"

Chapter 9

When Boobs and Doc entered Swindle's suite, he sprang up on the side of the bed and howled, "Damn, don't scare me like that. You know Jones is going to fall asleep as soon as he finishes his ice cream, and I'll be alone with those smelly people you sent up here."

"No, Bernie dear, we are not going to leave you alone. We're supposed to meet these people here to go over a little sting the good doctor is setting up to catch your lady love from Ipanema."

Big Boy Jones stopped eating, wiped the ice cream off his face, and said, "They're in yonder," pointing to the other room.

Noticing how distressed Swindle was, Doc suggested that Boobs stay with him and let Big Boy Jones go downstairs and eat supper.

This sounded fine to Big Boy, who got up with a great deal of difficulty and slowly waddled out the door.

With that, Dr. Suggs went next door and met the people Turner had sent. The short, slightly built Hispanic went by the name of Sancho, and the tall, muscular one called himself Ramon. Doc thought, *Sancho and Ramon who?* But he didn't ask, for fear they might be some paid assassins who worked for Turner. The huge black guy was named Eldridge. He asked the Arabic-looking man who was smoking a clove-scented cigarette if he was Muhammed. He assured him that he was. He then asked where the Arab girl was.

Muhammed chuckled and said, "There's been a slight delay. We couldn't get anything that smelled like burned camel dung and goats, so she had to go to the zoo to get some to soak her clothes with."

Doc was becoming more nervous by the moment, if that was possible, and asked Muhammed how long he thought it would take her, since he was in a hurry to get this ordeal behind him.

Muhammed said he didn't know, removed his cell phone, and dialed her. "Where are you, dummy, and how long will it take to get here? We are in room 711." He closed his cell phone.

"She'll be here momentarily."

Muhammed handed Doc a fez to put on and some dark sunglasses. He removed his tie and placed an amplifier on his neck to help disguise his high-pitched, squeaky voice, and he wrapped a black-and-gold ascot around it.

Dr. Suggs asked what that was for.

"Mr. Gibbs, this is to help disguise your voice. Anyway, we can't have you running around wearing a brown fedora. This will make things more realistic."

Dr. Suggs looked in the mirror and thought, *Hmm, not so bad, not so bad. My goodness, I hope these people are not as bad as Turner.*

Muhammed smiled as he took out another clove-scented cigarette and lit it.

Sancho asked them to hurry up and get on with it.

While they were rehearsing the plan, there was a disturbance in the other room. None of the people knew what was going on, but Doc had his suspicions, particularly when he heard Swindle whining, "For God's sake, mama, don't squeeze me so hard. I promise I'll never do it again."

Things had reached a point where Doc knew one thing for sure: if he got out of this mess and things worked out all right, he was going to cut his ties with Swindle and Turner.

When Swindle continued to holler and they heard several loud slaps, Doc reentered Swindle's room and asked them to tone it down until they got through.

"I thought you said you were going to wait until you got home before you spanked him."

Boobs didn't seem to be enjoying what she was doing to Swindle, frowned, and tersely replied, "I'm trying to, but he won't let me. What happened to your voice?"

About that time, Doc was distracted by a knock on the door. He managed to focus his eye in order to see through the door's security peephole. On the other side of the door, he saw a heavyset Arabic-looking woman and quickly decided this was the woman they were waiting for and let her in. She smelled like burned camel dung and singed goat.

When Swindle smelled her, he shouted, "Hot damn, this woman smells like shit to me. What's going on around here, good doctor? Your voice sounds like a frog croaking, and who in the hell are those people?"

Dr. Suggs looked at him and, for the first time in quite some time, smiled and said, "Don't worry, counselor, everything is fine. Now you and Miss Boobs calm down while we go next door and get everything set up."

"What in the hell are you setting up?" Swindle asked.

"You'll find out in due time, counselor. I think it's a good plan, and if you don't believe me you can ask Miss Boobs."

Boobs looked perplexed. She didn't have any idea what Doc was doing but said, "If you say so, good doctor, if you say so. Now calm down, Bernie, mama's gonna look after you."

Doc sent the Arabic woman next door, where they could run through the skit before leaving for the tenth floor.

Dr. Suggs lagged behind long enough to beg Boobs and Swindle again to refrain from what they were doing. "My goodness, Miss Boobs, quit before you completely turn him into a squalling infant."

"Boobs asked, "Do you need a cough drop?"

"No, I'm wearing a voice amplifier." Exasperated, he turned and left.

When they had completed the skit, they left for Roho's room. Sancho was somewhat of a prankster who seemed to be carried away with the prospects of what they planned to do. He picked up a tray that had been left in the hall for room service to pick up. When he approached Roho's door, he knocked and said, "Room service, madam," in his Spanish accent.

This threw Roho off guard, and she got up and came to the door. "I didn't order room service."

"Nice lady, Carlos sent it."

When Sancho said that, she was completely carried away by the prospect of seeing Carlos and opened the door. The minute she opened it she saw the short man with the fez on his bald head wearing dark sunglasses, the two perfumed Hispanics, and the Arabic man and woman who smelled like they had just left a tent in the Arabian desert somewhere.

She panicked, started cursing, and lunged at them in an effort to try to get out the door. When she did, the huge black man, Eldridge, who had remained in the hall, grabbed her and held her so tight that she couldn't move.

She lashed out at them in Spanish, stating, "You worthless bastards, get out of here before I call security."

Eldridge calmly replied in his deep baritone voice, "OK, ho, you just do that. We've got business with you. We are the only security you got."

Sancho, who did most of the talking for the Hispanics, smiled and said, "That's right, bitch, we've got business with you." He pointed to Dr. Suggs and smiled. "Mr. Gibbs here is in charge, and he's going to call all the shots."

Muhammed, who had been silent, piped up and spoke to the Arabic woman. "Before we start, dummy, would you remove the ring from her right hand? It's my understanding that it may contain some foreign substance." The reason he said "foreign substance" was that none of them knew for sure that it contained poison.

Dummy removed it, gently placed it in a handkerchief, and gave it to Doc, who put it in a small plastic bag and handed it to Ramon.

Roho kicked at Eldridge and Sancho and shouted angrily, "You don't know what you're in for. I have friends on the way."

With that, Ramon took out a roll of duct tape and none too gently wrapped her wrists and legs. Eldridge helped him spread her out and tape her to the bed.

Dr. Suggs spoke up. "Dear, we're here to make some money. Now don't hold your breath waiting on Carlos, if that's the one you're thinking about. It's my understanding that he is entertaining three young ladies who are presently working in the Peace Corps. He has long since forgotten about you. Now don't get too upset, because we've all been dropped at one time or another. As I was saying earlier, we're here to make some money, and you're going to help us. By the way, who hired you to kill that big fat lawyer you were with yesterday? Whoever did is no doubt wealthy—at least that's my understanding. All we know about her, thus far, is she goes by the name of Jenny and has light-brown hair. Would you care to elaborate on it?" he asked in his gravelly, amplified voice.

"No, you old bastard. You're not going to get anything out of me."

Sancho interrupted and said, "Mr. Gibbs, me and Ramon take her and work her on the streets. No telling how many tricks she can turn. That way, we can get some money."

This seemed to shock Roho.

Doc turned, rubbed his chin, and said, "Señor, we're not here to get chicken feed, we're here to get real money. Now that can be one of the options, but let's run through the others. If push comes to shove we can do as you say once she's thoroughly addicted to cocaine. She can become your whore here in Chicago until she wears out."

"When no longer any good, what would you propose to do with her?" Ramon asked. "We can't let her go, you know."

Sancho smiled and said, "Strip her clothes off, drop her in sewer when she wear out. Why you ask?"

Dr. Suggs replied, "That's certainly a last resort. Muhammed, what do you think? Of course, I hope she cooperates."

"Mr. Gibbs, get Eldridge to take her clothes off so we can examine her. I might be able to sell her to a harem if she's not too used up already. Of course, when her owner gets tired of her, he'll no doubt sell her to someone else."

The Arabic woman, who was acting as if she could not talk, moaned and pulled on Muhammed's sleeve and motioned for a piece of paper on which she wrote down something that was completely irrelevant to the matter at hand.

"That's right, dummy, we can always sell her for six goats to a herdsman up in Kyrgyzstan or Afghanistan. That is, after she's been circumcised. They always like to alter their women so they'll know they won't be running around on them."

Dummy grabbed his arm again, shook it, and wrote something in Arabic on a piece of paper.

Muhammed said, "Oh, right, right. We'll no doubt have to fatten her up because they like fat women who are very fertile, in addition to being circumcised."

By now they were beginning to get Roho's attention, because she was starting to tremble and it wasn't from being naked in the cold room.

Dr. Suggs intervened again, held up his hands in front of Muhammed, and said, "Muhammed, that's well and good. How much money can we get for six goats? We don't need any goats. That wouldn't bring in enough money to pay for one night in this room."

"I know, I know. I just say that could happen as a last resort. We could sell her for six goats to some old man who needs another wife, since she probably has been used by many men. Check the room to see if she has enough money to go by boat, if we can't sell her to a harem."

Dummy shook his arm again and made some symbol in Arabic. "Or, as a last resort, we could sell her as a concubine to a bunch of nomads in Afghanistan or someplace," Muhammed casually said.

Dr. Suggs intervened again. "You're not keeping your eye on the ball. We want the money. We need to know who sent her here. Of course, all those options are open in case she won't tell us what we need to know. Personally, I'm sure that she'd rather talk, and we'd rather she would, because we can split the so-called Jenny-with-the-light-brown-hair's fortune with this tramp and let her go."

Roho reared up and yelled, "Kill me, I don't care!"

Dr. Suggs peeped over at her and said, "I'm sorry, dear, we can't allow you to take the easy way out. It's going to be one of the options we mentioned. Now if you take the right one and lead us to who paid you to get rid of the lousy attorney, there can be a good outcome for all of us. Considering what I know about you, you're pretty dumb when it comes to being a good Communist in that you don't have what it takes to be a good Marxist. You know as well as I do that you couldn't subjugate yourself to the role of a fellow traveler, either in California where you originated, Peru, Brazil, or even in the Soviet Union. I would say that you have quite a problem. Now think about it for a minute. We can come up with more options, but the ones mentioned are probably enough: ending up in a sewer dead in a short time after you've been used up in Chicago, being some poor man's circumcised wife in Kyrgyzstan, or being passed around as a concubine. Of course, you could live a very prosperous life and continue to learn a little bit more about Marxism, since you seem to know very little about it and are certainly not very dedicated."

"I'm sure you would prefer to get half of this particular person's money and spend it going around lecturing about how good Marxism and Maoism and all those isms are to all the elitists in the so-called civilized world. Now the choice is yours, Miss Roho."

With that, Dr. Suggs turned and looked at the group and asked what they thought.

Sancho was the first to speak. "I can always find whores, so if she will make the right choice I'll gladly go out and get another one tonight. If not, I'll take her until she wears out and then dump her."

Muhammed replied, "I'll try to sell her to a sheikh, but I don't think I can because she's been used too much. I guess we'll have to circumcise her and fatten her up and sell her to some poor soul as a wife or a concubine. Of course, I prefer what you said earlier, Mr. Gibbs, about sharing this Jenny's fortune with us. Half for this stupid bitch, half for us, and nothing for this Jenny who paid her to kill that attorney."

While they were talking, the frightened Roho was thinking about how she could go about getting away. Should she divulge who had hired her or at least who she thought had hired her and later try to make an escape, or what?

Dr. Suggs interrupted the silence and looked at Sancho. "You know, this stupid pseudo-Marxist is trying to think. Right now I bet she's running through all the options in her mind and trying to figure out which one of us would offer her the best chance to escape her fate."

Sancho replied, "No way, man, no way. She can't escape. I hope the bitch is not stupid enough to think she can escape. She might have been to college, but she's still a stupid bitch with no street smarts."

He made those comments to try to make her angry and at the same time frighten her.

Dummy pulled on Muhammed's sleeve and wrote something else down in Arabic. After glancing at it, he shook his head and said, "No, not now. If it comes down to that when we sell her, they can do it then."

Doc looked at him and asked, "What did she tell you?"

"Oh, she asked if we would cut her tongue out like they did Dummy's for not obeying her master. I told her whoever ended up with her could do whatever they want."

Muhammed lit another clove cigarette and blew smoke in Roho's face. "Woman, what will it be? Mr. Gibbs may be slightly built, but he does not have any patience. Can't you see how he's becoming tense? You should make up your feeble mind while all the options are still open."

Doc asked Muhammed if he would get the Arabic woman to examine Roho to see how much flesh she needed to put on her if she ended up being sold as a concubine or as a poor man's wife.

Dummy, who smelled like camel dung or goats and who was acting like she couldn't speak, approached and started to feel Roho from head to foot.

Roho put up very little resistance. This led Dr. Suggs to believe that she was about ready to cooperate.

Eldridge, who had been quiet for quite some time, spoke up. "OK, ho, it's time to go. What is it going to be? I need the money. I can always work you as a ho just like these damn spics over here," he said, referring to Ramon and Sancho. "Of course, I'll be easier on you than they are. You might last four or five years, but there's one thing for sure, you won't get away. Now don't mess around with me. I want the damn money, and Mr. Gibbs here wants the money. We don't care what happens to you. If we get the money, things will work out. Now, who was it that sent you to kill the attorney?"

Roho asked for a sip of water. Ramon pulled out a bottle of wine laced with cocaine and offered her a drink. "This is all you can drink for now. You've got to get used to drinking wine and using drugs."

She took a large swallow, causing her heart to start pounding.

Sancho turned to Dr. Suggs and asked, "Mr. Gibbs, when she gets a little higher, if she doesn't come through, can we all have our way with her before we decide on the other options?"

Doc raised his hands and said, "I don't think it will come to that. She's ready to go. Now where to, Miss Roho?"

At first she didn't make a move. She just lay there shaking, with her heart pounding like her chest was about to explode.

Dummy pulled on Muhammed's sleeve and wrote something down.

He replied, "You can show her how we do it, but don't do it. We haven't gotten to that point yet, and we don't want her bleeding on the bed."

When he said that, Dummy pulled out a sharp stone, and Muhammed asked Eldridge and Ramon to spread her legs a little more while Dummy tickled her clitoris with the stone. This caused Roho to start to hyperventilate.

Doc asked Dummy to restrain herself. He then looked at the group and said, "Folks, I'll tell you what. I'll do away with all of y'all if I have to, but I want Roho to take us to the person who took out the contract on the attorney. I don't know the person's correct name. I just know she is wealthy. But I'm sure we can find out. There are a lot of options open to us, isn't that right?" He smiled at Roho as he spoke.

After experiencing the rush from the cocaine and the threat of castration, Roho started to talk incessantly using very proper English.

"I know where the money was wired from in France, and I know the name of the bank. The woman who placed the order went by the name of Jenny. Can I really get half of her money if I lead you to the woman who wanted the lawyer killed?" she frantically asked, thinking all the time that she would try to escape somewhere along the way.

"That's precisely what can happen, my dear," Dr. Suggs replied. "Now you're beginning to sound somewhat less stupid. I'm sure Muhammed can accompany you to France. My goodness, we must get the papers ready. Sancho, can you get the papers together for us?"

"Yes, Mr. Gibbs, yes."

"I'm glad we've got this sorted out," Doc sarcastically said as he turned to Roho. "Aren't you, my dear? Just think, we'll all come out of this with a considerable amount of money. Personally, I'd prefer to have ours in Swiss francs rather than euros, but either will be fine. Now, you let Dummy help you get dressed so you and Muhammed can leave as soon as you quit shaking," he said as he looked at his watch and left the room.

Chapter 10

Doc was appalled when he walked into Swindle's suite and caught him lying face down with his trousers around his ankles and Boobs bent over him, thrashing him with his belt. With his heart racing and panting for breath, Doc weakly uttered, "Good grief, Miss Boobs, stop, stop, stop. I thought you said you were going to wait until you got home before you gave him a spanking."

She was startled when she saw the disgusted old man and nervously tried to smile before answering. "I'm sorry, good doctor, but Bernie kept asking for it."

Doc couldn't figure out why in the world any sane person Swindle's age would ask for a spanking. "Would you please," he pleaded, "wait until you get to the privacy of his home to do such an outlandish thing?"

Boobs stopped, pulled up Swindle's trousers, and when he turned over to face Doc, he noticed Swindle's face was beefy red.

He couldn't help but think, *What in the world is happening here? Has this been going on since Swindle was a small child, or did it just start after he moved in with Miss Boobs? If I ever get out of this place, I'll guarantee one thing, I'll never get involved in anything like this again. It is bad enough what we are doing to Roho. There's no telling what they're going to do to her. I just hope they follow orders and no one gets hurt.*

Swindle whined, "I'm sorry, good doctor, it won't happen again. I just trust that you won't divulge our little secret."

Dr. Suggs stared at the ceiling and thought, *How could I? This is something I want to forget. In fact, I want to forget the whole thing, and as soon as we can get this straightened out, I'm going to be gone. Being in jail with Mertis and having*

Miss Fannie Kate after me is better than this. Why do I let people talk me into doing what I do?

Boobs handed Swindle his belt, told him to put it on, and crossed the room to where Dr. Suggs was. She removed his dark glasses and sweetly said, "Did you get things worked out, good doctor?"

"They are to some extent. I don't know exactly how yet. Do we have to go into it now? I think I'm about to drop dead from what I've just witnessed."

Boobs immediately thought he was referring to the spanking episode he had witnessed, but that wasn't the case. He was thinking about the scenario he and Turner's crew had set up. It was true, Swindle deserved something for doing what he had done with Roho, the so-called girl from Ipanema, but spanking at his age? No, he didn't think so. He had to be a very sick masochist.

When he failed to speak for quite some time, Boobs asked him if he needed a glass of water or to just sit down.

Without saying a word, he went into the bathroom and stuck his head under the faucet in the sink and ran water over it. It was true that he dreaded getting old, but if getting old meant that he wouldn't be around long enough to see what happened to some of the people in Swindle's generation, so be it. Some things seemed to be worse than death.

When he reached up to get a towel to dry his face, he noticed Boobs standing behind him, taking off her blouse. Thinking there was no telling what she had planned, he said, "What the heck are you doing?"

"Nothing, good doctor, I'm just going to take a shower. I'm all sweaty from the ordeal with Bernie and what I've been through. I just wish he would grow up and become a man. It seems that he doesn't understand, after all the years I've worked with him, that he is going to lose everything if anyone other than you and the women I pick for him find out about his behavior."

Doc wanted to tell her that she could rest assured that no one would find out from him, but he didn't. He just cleared his throat, turned, went into the other bedroom, and took a seat facing the window. How he wished for some moon pies and an RC Cola or maybe a half dozen Twinkies or Ding Dongs, since there were no hamburgers around like Miss Ailene's. His thoughts about Twinkies, Ding Dongs, and Ailene's burgers were interrupted when Boobs entered the room wrapped in a towel and asked him to hand her the bag she had purchased so she could get her underwear.

He spoke out in his now-gravelly, amplified voice, "Good heavens, gal, get some clothes on. Don't you know I can't take much more of what I've been through since we left Hooker County?"

She smiled at him and said, "What's the matter? Haven't you seen a lot of nude bodies in your time?"

He turned back toward the window and mumbled almost incoherently, "Yes, ma'am, but never like this."

She reached for her bag and took out the underwear she had purchased. After stepping into the panties and fastening the bra, she asked him if he would mind fetching the pantsuit that was folded over the back of a chair in the bathroom since the floor was slick.

He minded, but if it would help her to get dressed quickly, he would certainly do it. He hastily got up and went to the bathroom and retrieved her pantsuit for her.

She sat on the edge of the bed, slipped it on, and said, "Bless your heart, you're a sweet little fella, and I hope I haven't damaged your impression of me. But, let's face it, I look at you as a father figure most of the time."

Doc couldn't help but wonder what she meant by most of the time. For heaven's sake, surely she wasn't trying to seduce him. If so, she was out of luck. In spite of what he had witnessed, he still liked Boobs because she had always been very nice to him.

Once she was dressed, she removed his hat, kissed him on top of his bald head, and seductively walked into the bathroom and retrieved the pair of cherry-red panties she had removed from his back pocket earlier and handed them to him. "Here, good doctor, you sweet old thing, these are for you. You never know when you might need these again, particularly when you and Mertis start playing poker again."

Without thinking, he stuffed the dirty underwear in his back pocket. He cleared his throat and said, "I certainly hope not, Miss Boobs. I think after what I've been through, I'm going to stop playing poker and kidding around with Mertis. Whether you know it or not, the only reason I was playing with her was to try and stop her from playing poker. I would like to see her reform. I think when I get home I'll do what she asked me. I'll find her some nice young man who will treat her right—that is, if that's what she really wants."

Boobs hugged him and said, "You're a real sweetie. Damn, why can't all men be like you? Is it true that you've never been to a topless joint?"

Doc sniffed, cleared his throat, and looked at her, making good eye contact. He answered, "No, ma'am, and I don't ever intend to."

When he said that, she squeezed him again and kissed him on the cheek. "You don't have to, with all the women you've got at home."

He coughed a couple of times and felt like he was about to faint. He mumbled, "I think I'm going to give that up also. It's not what you think. We're just, um, I'm not sure how to put it. We're just bosom buddies. I guess that's as good a way as any to put it."

With that, the anxious old man turned and said, "Miss Boobs, if it's all right with you, I think I'll step outside and get some fresh air—that is, if there's any fresh air in this city."

Boobs, acting as if nothing unusual had happened, figured that this old country doctor had lived a rather sheltered life, except for going with several women in Hooker County, and had never witnessed what she had done to Swindle. She wanted to tell him that the only person she had ever spanked had been Swindle. Other than that, she was straight as an arrow, except for being a topless dancer who enjoyed the company of Jessica James.

When Doc passed back through Swindle's room, he couldn't face him. He made his way to the door, only to be stopped when Swindle shouted out in his deep baritone voice, "Good doctor, I want you to forget that what you saw really happened."

Doc turned, stared down at the floor, and replied, "As far as I'm concerned, counselor, I haven't even been to Chicago unless Mertis tells someone. My mind is going to be blank regarding this. I guess you could call it a prolonged senior moment." Without waiting for a response from Swindle, he opened the door and left.

Chapter 11

WHEN DOC GOT ON THE elevator, he saw Roho and Muhammed, arm in arm. Sancho and Ramon were babbling to each other in Spanish, and Eldridge and Dummy were standing silently in the back of the elevator.

At first, he was too frightened to speak.

Eldridge spoke first in his deep voice. "Mr. Gibbs, everything is worked out. Muhammed is taking over from here."

All Doc could say was "Good, good. Where are you going, Muhammed? I hope it's to the south of France, for everyone's sake."

"Yes, sir, Mr. Gibbs. We're headed to Paris and then on to the south of France. This is going to be a rather lucrative endeavor, unless our friend here fails to cooperate."

When they got off on the first floor, he bid them farewell and immediately went to the restaurant and ordered the largest steak on the menu.

The waiter asked how he wanted his steak and what he wanted with it.

Dr. Suggs nervously replied, "I want it well-done, with some Worcestershire sauce and four fried eggs sunny-side up and a pot of black coffee." He was on an anxiety-driven eating binge.

The waiter looked at him as if he was crazy and said, "Coming right up, sir. Would you like a drink beforehand?"

Dr. Suggs wanted to tell him that he would prefer to have the coffee now but didn't. He was still preoccupied with what he had just witnessed. He only hoped that he never saw any of them again after he got home. Although Boobs had her faults and Swindle was certainly a very strange crooked individual, he felt that they were the best of the lot. Why had he gotten himself mixed up with Turner? General Higgins's wife, Frances, had been right from the start;

he should have never messed with Turner. He hoped that they would find the Jenny with the light-brown hair, get their money, and let Roho go. It was true he felt that they should all pay for their bad behavior, either here on earth or later on, but he didn't want anyone to die. He wondered if Muhammed would do as he had been instructed or if he would get rid of Roho and Jenny with the light-brown hair. Maybe he should call Turner to be sure. Then again, he thought, *What the heck, I'm already neck deep in alligators. I'll just have to wait and see what happens.*

His silent musings were interrupted by Big Boy Jones, who came waddling over to his table, belched, and asked how things were going.

Doc sniffed and cleared his throat. "They are gone. Why don't you go back upstairs and stay with Mr. Swindle and ask Miss Boobs to join me in the restaurant?"

Jones, who didn't particularly like the idea of taking orders from the doctor, mumbled something to himself and left.

Chapter 12

When his meal arrived, he asked for Worcestershire sauce, causing the waiter to become incensed.

"Sir, we serve our steaks perfectly. Why would you want to ruin a steak with some sort of sauce?"

Dr. Suggs caught himself in a dilemma and said the first thing that came to his mind. "The Worcestershire sauce is for the eggs. How does that sound?"

"Very good, sir, if you say so. I just don't want to get the cook mad at me by thinking that someone would need to put something like that on one of the steaks he's prepared."

"Well, tell him he doesn't have to worry because everything is fine," Doc said as he reached in his pocket and gave him a fifty dollar bill. "My compliments to the chef, sir."

About the time he started to eat, Boobs walked in and sat down next to him rather than on the other side of the table. When the waiter came over to the table, she asked him if he would mind bringing her a Caesar salad and another plate to put part of Doc's steak on, since she didn't think he would be able to eat it all by himself.

The waiter couldn't help but think, *These Southern folks are strange.* He kept his thoughts to himself and turned to go get her a Caesar salad and the additional plate.

While she was waiting for the salad, her better side didn't mention anything that had happened in Swindle's suite. She could only think to thank him for accompanying her to Chicago to help save Swindle.

Doc cut off a large bite of steak doused in Worcestershire sauce, placed it in his mouth, and started to chew. He had run out of things to say and only wanted to eat.

She became uncomfortable with his silence and asked if she could have a bite. He cut off a small portion and handed it to her on his fork, and she started to eat.

When the Caesar salad arrived, she continued to talk and told him her life story.

He couldn't help but wonder why she was telling him. He didn't need to know, but listened anyway. It seemed that she had run away from home because her stepfather had tried to molest her when she was in the eighth grade and had been on the road ever since. Oddly enough, she had not been promiscuous, as best he could tell. She had worked as a waitress and accumulated enough money to purchase a used trailer that someone wanted to leave behind, because it would cost too much to move, and had started her own topless joint, the Purple Pussy Cat. This was when she met Swindle, and her life drastically changed. It seemed she felt sorry for Swindle, had taken him under her wings, and had tried to rehabilitate him after old man Bigelow had fired him and chased him out of town.

The only fault Doc could come up with was she loved to help Swindle sue large corporations and run topless joints, health clubs, and massage parlors. He was somewhat shocked to learn that their existence together had never been sexual. In fact, she didn't particularly care about men.

She went on to say that she wished she could have had him for a father, as things could have been different.

He thought, *I'm not so sure about that after what happened between me and my promiscuous wife and her two girls.*

In spite of what he felt about the wife's greedy girls, he said, "I would have put you back in school, and you could have gone on and done anything you wanted to do. After all, you're the one with the brains, not Mr. Swindle, even though you only have an eighth-grade education."

Boobs blushed, thanked him for the nice compliment, and said, "As soon as we get through eating, we've got to wrap up a few loose ends."

Chapter 13

When they finished eating, Doc paid the bill and they made their way to the elevator, only to have Boobs again bring up the possibility of him adopting her and becoming her father.

His jaw dropped when he realized she was serious. *What in the world is this woman talking about? Me adopting her? Why?* "You must be kidding, Miss Boobs. Why would you wish to be adopted? You have a father, and in fact you said you had a stepfather until you left home."

Boobs became tearful and somberly said, "I don't have a father. Mother named me Hortense Doe, since she had to put something on my birth certificate and that lousy stepfather who tried to abuse me would not adopt me. I'm not asking for much. I'd like to just think that I could really have a last name, and knowing you and how straitlaced you are, I can't think of a person whose last name I'd rather carry."

The way she said it had Doc feeling like he was overburdened with the responsibility to do something. He couldn't help but think, *I can't afford to let my deceased mother cause me to do something like this. I think that's about the only thing she didn't instruct me to do in order to try to make women happy.*

When they got off the elevator on the security floor, Boobs dropped down to her knees, placed her arms around his hips, and started to beg. "Would you please seriously consider it? I'll never cause you any trouble. I'll only call on you when I need advice and visit you on holidays and special occasions. Aw heck, I'll just stop by anytime just to see you, if it's okay with you. No one has to know, except the two of us."

Dr. Suggs not only thought about the fact that the cameras were on and that they were being recorded, but that here was this fine young woman who had her faults, down on her knees begging him to, of all things, adopt her.

Somewhat panicky and not wanting to hurt her feelings, he said as he tried to remove her hands from his hips, "My goodness, don't you realize that Henry and Collette may be watching us? What do you think they will think you're trying to do?"

"I don't care. I'm not trying to do anything other than to get you to consider what I've asked. Will you give me a name?"

"Why me?"

"Because, just like I told you. You're a nice person and it won't cost you a thing and I'll never cross you. I won't treat you like your family did."

When she said that, Doc felt a surge of anger, grabbed her hair and pulled it gently, and said, "Enough, that's enough. Now get up, Miss Boobs. We can talk about this later. Right now we have to go settle up with our two lovebirds, dear sweet Henry and his insatiable French lover."

Chapter 14

THEY WERE BOTH EMOTIONALLY SPENT by the time they reached security, knocked on the door, and called Collette to let them in.

She flittered over, opened the door, smiled, and said, "Come in, Mr. Gibbs, we've been looking for you and your associate. What did you say her name was?"

"Doe, my name is Doe," Boobs said authoritatively in an effort to establish who was in control of the situation.

Collette smiled and said, "If you say so."

Dr. Suggs realized that something needed to be said, and in an effort to get these two off the topic of Boobs's last name, he asked, "Where's Henry? We need to settle up for now, if it's all right with y'all. Wouldn't you say so, Dominick?" He looked at Boobs.

Boobs seemed startled by the fact that he called her Dominick, but she made no comment.

Collette failed to pick up on this and smiled. She said, "Oh, Henry's in the break room resting. Today's been quite an ordeal, if you know what I mean."

Boobs commented, "It certainly has been quite a day," referring to all they had been through and how she and Henry had been carrying on.

"Shall we go in the break room and see if what we agree on is all right with Henry?" Boobs asked.

Collette made a slight effort to keep them out of the break room, only to have Dr. Suggs ease by her and open the door.

There was Henry, stretched out on the couch with his trousers and underwear down, his feet dangling off the side, and a half-eaten slice of pizza lying on his naked abdomen.

Doc, who had heard and seen about all he thought he could tolerate, asked Collette and Boobs if they would mind pulling up Henry's trousers as he removed the pizza. Sluggishly, Henry assisted them and finally managed to slowly get up and sit on the side of the couch.

Doc and Boobs took a seat on either side of him, and Collette sat on the floor between his legs, placed her arms around his waist, and hugged him.

"Henry, I hated to disturb your nap, but they wanted to settle up with us. You know, so we can complete the plans for our trip to Paris."

Henry mumbled, "Yes, dear, if you say so. Are you sure we can get off?"

"Absolutely. Now quit being so coy."

Doc, who by now was tired of everything he had witnessed during the last several hours, said, "Well, folks, Dominick and I need to be moving on, and we'd like to settle up for right now."

"For right now!" Henry exclaimed.

"Yes, Henry. It could well be that we will need your services later on. Isn't that right, Dominick?"

"Yes, Mr. Gibbs. Is it all right if I show them some of our photographs?"

"Certainly, my dear," Doc answered.

With Doc's permission, Boobs reached in her purse and pulled out the Polaroid pictures she had made of them making love on the couch. Collette thought they looked very good and asked if she could have a copy. Henry, who by now was such a frightened, addled young man, said nothing.

"Sure, you and Henry can keep them in your scrapbook. I trust that things are going to work out well between the two of you," Boobs said with a certain amount of sarcasm.

Collette was quick to reply. "Henry is coming along, and I'm sure that things are going to work out just fine."

Doc sniffed a couple of times, cleared his throat, and changed the topic. "Now, folks, you certainly have enough money to make it to Paris, and with another couple of thousand dollars you can have a good time. In fact, I guess you've been having a good time without the money and without going to Paris, but it should be much more romantic there than it is here—since here you have to worry about the manager or someone coming in and catching you. Now take this two thousand dollars."

Collette squeezed Henry around the waist again and said, "Oh, darling, you might not have been my first, but you will be my last."

After that tender remark, Boobs and Doc had seen and heard enough and stood and headed for the door. Dr. Suggs said, "Good, folks, y'all have a nice trip."

Boobs, having recovered somewhat from her earlier conversation with Dr. Suggs about adopting her, said as they turned to leave, "Collette, you must remember that you've got to go a little slower until you've gotten Henry broken in the way you want him."

Chapter 15

On the way to Swindle's suite, Boobs asked Doc, "Where did you come up with this 'Dominick' business? You caught me totally off guard, and I just hope I reacted to your new name for me without causing any suspicion. Did you just run through a list of names that you thought might suit me?"

Doc noticed from the tone of her voice that she wasn't very happy with him calling her Dominick. He haltingly replied, "I can't really say. It could have been that it just popped into my mind, so to speak. You know, since you've been functioning as a dominatrix for Mr. Swindle."

"What the hell do you mean?"

"Miss Boobs, that's a woman who physically and psychologically dominates and abuses her partner in a sadomasochistic way. In other words, when it comes to Swindle you're a dominating woman, so to speak."

She didn't care for this description of her and tartly replied, "Don't you ever call me that again."

"I won't," Dr. Suggs passively mumbled, "as soon as you stop indulging in such behavior."

Boobs uncharacteristically blushed and acted as if she was really hurt by what he had said and informed him that this would be Swindle's last spanking by her.

"Good, now let's drop the subject, Miss Boobs—I mean Hortense."

"What's the matter with you? You know I don't like Hortense. Like I told you, my thoughtless mother just had that put on my birth certificate."

Doc knew what he had said was out of character for him and said, "How about if I get Judge Spence to help us come up with a solution?"

"Say," Doc said as he turned and looked up at her, "how about Renee?"

"I don't know. I don't know many people named Renee, and just what kind of name is that?"

"How should I know? It just sounded good to me. Now come on and let me bid adieu to Mr. Swindle. I've got to make arrangements to follow up on what our actor friends have done with Roho and see if they've found Jeanie with the light-brown hair."

When they opened the door, Swindle almost bounded out of the bed. He could just see Marta Roho returning for a final visit.

Big Boy Jones, who was sleeping in a chair by the television, didn't budge.

Doc calmly said, "Calm down, Mr. Swindle, things are looking up. We now have Roho under control, and we're in the process of locating Jenny with the light-brown hair or whoever sent Roho here to get rid of you."

Frightened, Swindle bellowed, "Whatta you mean, you've got Roho under control? Where is she, and who is this Jenny with the light-brown hair? She might pay someone else to come after me, since that Latin firecracker failed."

Boobs sat on the bed next to Swindle and said, "I want to clarify one other thing for you. I am not going to spank you again."

"Whatta you mean?" he moaned.

"Exactly what I said. I'm not going to do it again. We'll have to think of something else to help you get the punishment you desire."

Dr. Suggs cleared his throat, sniffed and snorted, and finally got around to saying, "Where is the tan alligator briefcase?"

Mr. Swindle hated to part with money, so he acted as if he didn't know.

Boobs started to slap him, and he begged for mercy before telling her it was under the bed. With that, she got down on her knees, retrieved the briefcase, and handed it to Dr. Suggs.

Swindle sheepishly asked, "Good doctor, what are you going to do with all that money? Do you plan to blow it all on food or something?"

Dr. Suggs, for the first time in many years, expressed himself extremely forcefully by answering, "I'm gonna blow it on bringing to a conclusion what you've gotten yourself into. If there's any left over, I'm going to give it to Jessica James to put back in your safe so you can entertain the public officials. How does that sound? In the meantime, I'll be gone for an unknown length of time."

"Where to?" Swindle shouted.

"To France."

"Why?"

"To save your blistered butt, I hope."

Chapter 16

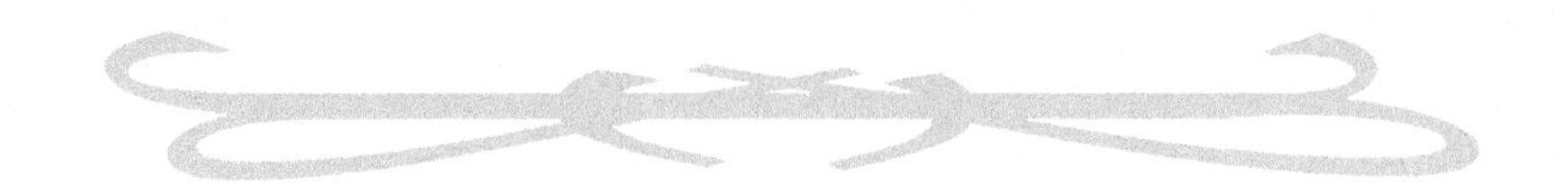

Doc took the tan alligator briefcase and turned to leave. Before he got out the door, Doc suggested that Swindle take his plane back home and, if they could get Big Boy Jones awake, let him drive the Bentley.

"What the hell do you mean?" Swindle asked.

"Exactly what I said, counselor. I'm going to catch the City of New Orleans."

"Hell, fella, somebody will snatch that briefcase full of money from you before you get out of the hotel, as old and feeble as you are."

When Swindle said that, Boobs shouted, "Shut up, Bernie, he knows what he's doing. Do I need to remind you that he's not the one who went with Marta Roho? You are, and you're the one that's in trouble! Hopefully he can get this thing settled."

Swindle developed a sad look on his face and said, "I'm sorry, good doctor. Take the briefcase and do whatever in the hell you want to with it, but I'm not about to let Big Boy Jones drive my Bentley home. I'll hire someone up here to do it or send for Jessica James to come up and drive it home."

"Suit yourself, counselor, suit yourself. Right now I'm in a hurry, since it's only an hour until the City of New Orleans leaves."

Boobs followed him out the door and asked, "What about me? What are you going to do for me?"

"Whatta you mean, what am I going to do for you, Miss Boobs? I'm going to give you a chance to walk the straight and narrow. Of course, that won't mean giving up your topless bars, but it will certainly mean not being a participant in all these frivolous lawsuits and acting as a dominatrix."

She slumped and looked down at the floor. "Fair enough, I'll see you when you get back. Where do you think you're going in France?"

"I'm not sure. I might end up in the south of France if I have to, but one way or another I'm gonna make sure we all get out of this with at least some modicum of integrity."

"I don't know what modicum means," Boobs replied feebly. "However, if it's all right with you, it's all right with me. Now have a safe trip, Daddy."

When she said Daddy, he dropped the briefcase and almost fell down. She rushed over to him, picked up the briefcase, and asked if he was all right.

Rather than telling her what he was thinking, he assured her that he would be fine shortly and not to worry.

This was the first time he had ever been called Daddy. Did she mean it, or was she kidding him?

She kissed him on the cheek with tears in her eyes and bid him farewell.

When he reached the lobby of the hotel, he called Turner again. Turner was becoming upset with him, calling so frequently. He said, "What is it this time?"

"One more thing and that'll be it. I need Eldridge to meet me at the train station and accompany me to New Orleans."

Turner curtly asked, "Damn, why do you need Eldridge to go to New Orleans?"

"That's just the beginning of the trip. I need him to accompany me all the way to the south of France. I've got to follow up on Roho and find the person who sent her to dispense with the attorney."

"Why?"

"Because I have to see for myself. That's why."

"Okay, but make up your mind. You should know that I can't afford to be taking calls all the time. You're gonna cause me to blow my cover."

Dr. Suggs cleared his throat before replying. "I'm sorry. I can assure you it won't happen again." And that ended their conversation.

Doc stood out in front of the hotel, waiting on a cab, and before one could arrive, Eldridge drove up to the curb in a blue Ford Taurus and growled out in his deep, baritone voice, "Get in, Mr. Gibbs. Why in the hell are we going to New Orleans on a train?"

Doc hated to tell him that he didn't fly and that he couldn't ride in a car and drive that far. "It's just the way I have to do it. Would you care to see what I have in this briefcase?" Dr. Suggs opened the briefcase just enough for Eldridge to see its contents.

Eldridge peeped over and noticed that the briefcase was full of thousand-dollar and hundred-dollar bills.

"Mr. Gibbs, I believe I understand completely. What's gonna be in it for us?"

Dr. Suggs mumbled, "Looks like a good bit to me, plus the amount of money Muhammed will get from the person who sent Roho here to assassinate the attorney."

"If you say so, Mr. Gibbs, we can always use a little extra money. Are you sure you don't want me to drive you to New Orleans?"

"Yes, I'm sure, young man. I don't want you to drive me to New Orleans. I want to ride the train just one more time before I die, and when we get to New Orleans, we're gonna get someone to falsify papers so we can catch a boat to Europe. You know, I haven't been on a boat since January of 1946 when I came back from the service."

Eldridge couldn't help but wonder if the old man was losing his wits and countered by saying, "If you say so. How long do you think we'll be gone?"

"I wish I could say, Eldridge. I can only say as long as it takes."

Dr. Suggs felt the urge to gorge himself on moon pies and asked if Eldridge knew where to find some.

Chapter 17

WHILE ELDRIDGE WAS ESCORTING DOC around Chicago to see if he could help him find a box of moon pies, Muhammed and Roho were on a flight to Paris.

Muhammed and Roho's flight to Paris was quiet—in fact, too quiet because when the plane landed, Roho made a break for it as soon as she saw two people who looked like airport security agents.

"Help! I'm being held against my will by that Arab," she yelled as she pointed to Muhammed.

The men hurried her out of the airport and into a car before she realized what was happening, and they gave her an injection of Valium. They then bound, gagged, and blindfolded her and drove to an isolated chateau fifty miles south of Paris.

When they arrived at their destination, she was stripped and placed in a dark, damp, eight-by-eight room after being given another injection of Valium.

When she slowly recovered from the Valium, she was so cold she started to moan and cried out for help.

After waiting another thirty minutes, a tall, thin, brown-haired, French-looking man, who appeared to be in his late thirties or early forties, entered the room and offered her a warm glass of cognac laced with cocaine. She drank it in two swallows.

A short time later, her heart started to pound and she felt as though she was about to die.

He stood over her and laughed before finally picking her up and dumping her in a sweatbox. She had only been in the sweatbox a few minutes when she started hearing Muhammed begging the two men to quit stretching him out on a rack and dripping acid on him and that he would gladly tell them why they were in France.

Muhammed told his two captors that he had accompanied her to France to meet a woman who was very wealthy and to collect some money. He moaned, "Please stop. I don't know where the money is. She does."

When Roho could tolerate it no longer, she screamed, "I think I'm going to die if I don't get out of here and cool off. That Muhammed character is lying. I don't know anything."

The other French-looking man, who was also in his forties, with salt-and-pepper hair and a thin mustache, opened up the box, smiled at her, and replied, "Mademoiselle, I know just the thing that will help you cool off and remind you why you are here. The fella that brought you over here says that you are here to collect some money. Now I need to know who this other person is. Muhammed, or whatever his name is, is about gone, and he doesn't seem to know."

Once out of the sweatbox, they placed her in a harness and lowered her into a dark, deep well. Not only was it dark, but the water was cold, and they allowed her to be submerged several times. When she wasn't submerged, she thrashed around, trying to keep her head above water, and begged for mercy.

The tall, thin man was quick to remind her that all could be reconciled as soon as she told them what they needed to know.

"Mademoiselle, the gentleman who brought you over here does not seem to know your destination. Anyway, we don't need him, and we will no doubt dispose of him in due time. However, your fate can be much better, provided you lead us to the woman who has the money. If you comply with our demands, you will be spared and rewarded to some extent."

By this time, Roho was totally confused, frightened, and thoroughly convinced that her options, for the time being, had run out. If she was to escape, it would have to be later. For the time being, she figured the best thing for her to do was to try to find the person who had ordered the killing of the attorney and relieve her of her money.

"Stop!" she screamed. "I will, I will!"

They brought her up from the well and let her shake on the cold stone floor before congratulating her for making a wise decision.

Chapter 18

THE TWO MEN TALKED BACK and forth to each other, without mentioning their names, about what they should do with Muhammed. Finally, they decided to wait until after they checked out Roho's story before disposing of him. In the meantime, they would leave him locked in his room with a gallon of water. If he needed anything else to drink, he could drink his urine. This frightened Roho to the point that she felt completely helpless.

When she started to recover, they bound her and dumped her in the backseat of the car, naked, and left for Nice. While en route, they reviewed with her several times exactly what she was to do, in order to make sure she understood.

A few miles outside of Nice she told them she needed to used the restroom. They figured this was some sort of ploy to try to get away, and told her to go ahead and use the bucket that was in the car.

She didn't like that one bit, but there was nothing she could do about it, so she went in the bucket. Even for her, this was an extremely humiliating experience.

When they arrived in Nice, they dressed her and she immediately took them to where the money had been wired to her group in Brazil. Throughout this ordeal she made no effort to escape; in fact, she was willing to go along with them at least to see what they would do after they found the person in question.

Once they located the bank where the transfer had been made to Carlos, they checked with the manager and told him that something had gone wrong and the transfer to Carlos had not cleared. The perplexed manager told them that it had cleared and if they had any questions they should check with Mrs.

Fox, who was staying in Cannes. He gave them her address, and they thanked the manager and departed.

They drove out into the countryside, took Roho out of the car, made her disrobe, tied her to the front of the car, and drove her around in a sparsely populated area until she became so cold that she passed out. They then placed her in the backseat of the car, naked, and headed for Cannes.

By the time they reached their destination, she was fully under their influence. Again, as earlier, they rehearsed how she and Madam Jenny Fox, as she called herself, would carry out the transaction at the bank. Not only would she remove the contents from her safe deposit box, but she would make several wire transfers to different corporations located in Panama, Monaco, and Luxembourg. She wanted to ask them about her part of the money and if they were going to release her, but she didn't. She figured she could wait.

Jenny Fox was shocked when they appeared at her door. They immediately seized her and told her that they wanted to help her out of an untenable situation.

She nervously asked what they were talking about.

The tall, thin man was quick to inform her that it was about saving her life, but it would no doubt cost her part of her money, since the lady who had accompanied them was the one whom she had hired to kill an attorney in Chicago.

She tried to act as if she didn't know what they meant, but it was obvious that she wasn't very good at acting, and they immediately tied up both women. They ran the tub full of cold water and dunked Jenny until she was ready to do anything they told her, while the frightened Roho observed.

The shorter of the two men, with the salt-and-pepper hair and the thin mustache, smiled and complimented her on making an excellent decision.

"You know, madam, half of something is better than nothing. Sooner or later we all wind up in the same place, but some people just make it there earlier than others."

Jenny, who was still shaking from the cold water and fear, asked, "What do you mean?"

The tall, thin man replied matter-of-factly, "You know that we all die. It's just a matter of when and how. We're offering you the opportunity to live longer if you do what we ask."

Roho, who had been quiet for some time, yelled at Jenny. "Damn you, bitch. You're the one that got me in this. Now you're going to get me out. There's no reason for either one of us to die."

"That's right," the short man said, and smiled. "There's no reason for anyone to die until their time comes."

As soon as Jenny and Roho made themselves presentable, they drove back to the bank in Nice, emptied the contents of her safe deposit box, and made the transfers. Rather than transferring all the money to one location, they transferred a large amount to each of the locations they had mentioned earlier and left a good bit in the bank in order to try to avoid suspicion.

They thanked the bank manager, gave him some papers and jewelry to be put in her safe deposit box, and left.

The two men decided after leaving the bank that they needed to stop and eat. Roho and Jenny were pleased to hear this. Not only were they hungry, but it might be a good time and place to escape. However, this would be deferred, since the two men restrained them and placed gags in their mouths and bags over their heads.

Chapter 19

ELDRIDGE AND DOC DIDN'T FIND the moon pies but were able to find some good barbecue on the south side of Chicago before making their way to the train station.

Once on the train, Doc devoured the barbecue like he was eating his last supper. This surprised the large Eldridge, who ate about a third as much as Doc did. He couldn't help but wonder how this small man could eat so much, but he didn't ask. Maybe the old man just wanted to make his last train ride, but be that as it may, Eldridge figured that he would be well compensated for the inconvenience.

When they finished eating they sat in the club car all the way to New Orleans and played poker. Dr. Suggs methodically beat Eldridge until he fell asleep.

Doc dreamed about Hooker County and all the good people who lived there. It wasn't the Garden of Eden, but certainly it was a nice place to live, because most of the people were very honorable.

When he awoke, he looked over at Eldridge and realized what he had always known—that there was no honor among people in his line of work. It wasn't whether they would cross you, but when. It was simply a matter of basic trust versus self-preservation. People like Turner had no basic trust, and if push came to shove, they always looked out for themselves. Doc hated to think such a thing, but deep down he knew it was true.

He thought, *That's why I'm going to France. I don't trust Muhammed and what Roscoe Turner's group plans to do with Marta Roho, the so-called Jenny with the light-brown hair, and who she might be working for. A promise is one thing, but ...*

When they arrived in New Orleans, he told Eldridge that they needed to go to the bank and rent a safe deposit box. Before they went in the bank, he opened the tan alligator briefcase again in order to let Eldridge have another look at the contents.

While Eldridge was sitting in the lobby of the bank, Dr. Suggs rented two safe deposit boxes—one for two months and another for one year. Certainly that would be long enough for what he had in mind. He placed the empty tan alligator briefcase and his papers in the safe deposit box he had rented for two months. In the other one, he placed most of the money except for two hundred thousand dollars, which he stuffed in his jacket pockets. He memorized the numbers and put the key to the one he had rented for a year under the insert in his right shoe.

Doc rejoined Eldridge in the lobby. He smiled at him and said in his amplified, gravelly voice, "Eldridge, my goodness, just think, we'll have this to split when we return." Doc held up the key to the safe deposit box he had rented for two months.

"You know, this plus what we get out of the trip will come in handy. Now all we need to do is make sure nothing happens to us. I would hate to see this not be part of the split."

Eldridge squinted and looked down at him. "Mr. Gibbs, now what exactly do you think might happen to us?"

"You know in this line of work there's no telling what can happen. That's why I only rented the box for two months."

Baffled, Eldridge replied, "Two months? Why two months, Mr. Gibbs?"

"Eldridge, my friend, if we're not back in two months we won't need any money, will we?"

"How's that?"

"Think about it, son. Some of your friends may dispose of us, or at least try to. You know how greedy people can get when money's involved, don't you?"

"Yes, sir, Mr. Gibbs. Yes, sir, I guess so."

"Before we pick up our forged papers, why don't we duck in a public restroom somewhere and split up some of the money I removed from the briefcase. We're gonna need a fair amount to make the trip. I can't wait to get this trip over so we can split the other money. Can you, Eldridge?"

"No, sir," Eldridge replied with a fair amount of uncertainty in his voice.

Chapter 20

AFTER PICKING UP THEIR FORGED papers and valise full of weapons, Doc told Eldridge he hoped he didn't mind traveling to England on a tramp freighter under Panamanian registry. It was obvious that Eldridge did mind, but he was caught between what he thought Turner would want him to do and what Doc was planning.

Doc wasn't particularly worried about being robbed by some of the human debris that were operating the ship, since not only was Eldridge a large man, but they both had quite a variety of weapons.

Once they arrived in Portsmouth, England, rather than renting a car, Doc bought a secondhand Volkswagen. After getting the papers straightened out, they headed for Dover. Doc didn't like tunnels much more than he liked the thought of flying, and they took the ferry across the English Channel.

Once across the channel, they drove nonstop to Paris and spent the night in a cheap hotel before meandering down to Marseille. Once in Marseille, Doc had no idea about what to do and where to go.

Doc asked, "Eldridge, did Muhammed give you any idea where he was going when he arrived in France?"

"No, sir, Mr. Gibbs. All I remember is hearing him say something to that ho about them going to Nice."

"I've never been to Nice. In fact, I've never been to France. What about you, Eldridge?"

"Not in a while," he gruffly said.

"How much money do you have left, Eldridge? I'm down to seventy-two thousand after the trip is over and buying this worthless secondhand Volkswagen."

Eldridge was slow to answer. "I think I've still got ninety-two out of the hundred thousand dollars you gave me."

"Good, my man, good. You know, with what we're going to get here and what's in that briefcase back in New Orleans, we should have enough money to take our time and enjoy the south of France. Whatta you think about going to Monaco?"

"Monaco? What the hell for?"

"Oh, well, it's not far out of our way," Dr. Suggs said while he was studying Eldridge's reaction.

"We ain't gonna do any gambling, are we, Mr. Gibbs?"

"No, not at all, son. We'll just rent us a good hotel room, have a couple of good meals, and look at the ladies strut on the beach. Whatta you think about that?"

"If you say so, Mr. Gibbs, but I kinda want to get this over with as quick as possible."

"How so, Eldridge?"

"I need to get back home."

"Where's home?" Dr. Suggs asked, hoping he would reveal a little more about his background.

"Chicago. At least that's where I've been hanging out for the last two years."

"You know, the other day was the first time I'd ever been to Chicago, Eldridge. I'm just an old country boy from way down south."

"You coulda fooled me, Mr. Gibbs. You talk like one and you walk like one, but you don't think like one—except for that train trip and the boat ride. Exactly what is your connection with the boss?"

Dr. Suggs lied. "I'm kinda like you. I'm not exactly sure, if you know what I mean, except we go back a while. Eldridge, are you gonna take the money we make from this and maybe go on an extended leave or something? You know, I plan to retire if everything works out all right. I'm an old man and don't have many more years left. I'm getting too old for this type of thing."

Eldridge looked over at him and frowned. "I don't know whether I believe you or not."

This startled Dr. Suggs, and he tried to remain calm before making a reply. "Why is that?"

"Because we've been together now for two weeks and you haven't told me a damn thing, except that we're going to France to see if we can't locate whoever took out the contract on the attorney and take their money. When are you gonna really let me in on exactly what your plans are?"

"Eldridge, like I said, we're going to Monaco for a day or two, and then we're going back to Nice to find out who's been there and where they're headed. Have you got any idea where they were headed after they left Nice?"

"All I know is that Muhammed knows some people in the Bordeaux region."

"Good. I wouldn't be at all surprised if that isn't where we end up, would you, Eldridge?"

"If you say so, Mr. Gibbs," a perplexed Eldridge answered.

Chapter 21

WHILE ELDRIDGE AND DOC WERE languishing in Monaco, trying to figure out who they needed to get in contact with in Nice or Cannes, the two men and their captives, Marta Roho and Jenny Fox, met Muhammed in Toulouse.

Roho was extremely surprised when she saw Muhammed smiling outside the farmhouse where he had been waiting on them to arrive.

She shouted out, "You lousy bastards, you lied. You said you were going to kill him. You are all in this together, aren't you?"

Muhammed smiled, showing his tobacco-stained teeth, and replied to her outbursts. "My, you finally got something right, my dear. My two friends, you, Jenny with the light-brown hair, and I have one more place to go before this is over. By the way, Jenny, what is your real name?"

Jenny, who had always been a spoiled brat, was not used to being around people like this, much less being stripped of her clothing and given the water treatment before going to the bank in Nice.

The tall, thin man looked over at her and said, "Oh, Muhammed, this is Jenny Fox, or so she says."

Roho started to squirm in an effort to break loose from the way she was tied and said, "You bloody bastards, you're going to pay if you harm me. I don't care what you do with this tramp." She was referring to Jenny. "Carlos and his comrades, in spite of what Mr. Gibbs told you, will catch up with you."

The short man with the salt-and-pepper hair and the thin mustache smirked and replied to her outburst. "Madam—I'm sure it's madam instead of mademoiselle—I rather doubt that your friend Carlos will be looking for you.

Don't you remember that Mr. Gibbs told Muhammed that he's now nesting with some young American girls who are in that Peace Corps thing?"

Before Roho could answer, Jenny started crying like she used to when she was in trouble and begged them to please let her go. "I don't care what you do to this woman, but I'm a very important person, and if you know what's good for you, you will release me right now."

Muhammed took a deep draw from his clove cigarette and sarcastically said, "Madam, I'm not aware that you have any friends left. Do I need to remind you that you just transferred most of your money to us, or at least to the group we represent? Now, Roho, here, I understand has some in a bank in Luxembourg. Maybe you can get her to share with you, since she is supposed to be a good Communist."

The tall, thin Frenchman laughed and replied, "Not really, she just thought she did. We transferred her part to one of the group's account. She is a lost whore in the south of France with nowhere to go unless you can think of something to do with her."

Muhammed thumped his cigarette out onto the dry, barren earth and smiled. "I know just the place."

Chapter 22

While Eldridge was preoccupied with watching the nude and topless girls on the beach, Doc was thinking about how they were going to find out how to locate Roho and Muhammed and, hopefully, the so-called Jenny with the light-brown hair.

It wasn't long before two young women, speaking Spanish, strolled by.

Doc called out to them and, much to his surprise, they came over to where he and Eldridge were seated. He didn't know quite how to say it, but he managed to ask if they wanted to make a little honest money. He was terribly afraid they were going to turn him in to the police for trying to solicit on a public beach, but he ran the risk.

The older of the two young women, who spoke broken English, asked, "What do you mean about making some honest money?"

"As you can no doubt tell, I'm not from around here, and I'm trying to locate my granddaughter, who has run away from home. It's my understanding that she was last seen at a bank in Nice with another woman and maybe one or two men."

The way he was talking to the young ladies confirmed to Eldridge that he wasn't an ordinary country bumpkin. The old man was an extremely sharp operator, and so he sat there and quietly observed.

Doc gave his name as Percy Gibbs and showed them his passport for more identification.

The older of the two asked, "Why did you stop us?"

"Because my granddaughter is part Spanish, and you reminded me of her," he said as he reached in his pocket and pulled out a picture of Roho. "By the way, am I correct? Where are you lovely ladies from?"

They gave him a shy grin and said, "Barcelona, Spain. We're only here for three more days and then go back home."

"Good. I'm sure you'll enjoy your stay. Maybe if you can help me locate my granddaughter, who was last seen in Nice, I can make it worth your while, so you can stay an extra couple of days if you have the time to spare."

They both informed him that they did have time to spare to help him find his granddaughter, for the right price.

He smiled at them, looked at Eldridge, and said, "Son, I believe we're making progress. It's amazing what a little money can do, isn't it?"

"Yes, sir, Mr. Gibbs. Yes, sir," Eldridge replied as he continued to eye the younger of the two women.

"Now just to show you that we're on the up-and-up, my friend here can stay with your friend," Doc told the older woman, "while you and I go to Nice. Or if you'd like, we can all four go to Nice. That is, if we can make some sort of suitable financial arrangement."

Doc reached in his pocket and took out one thousand dollars. "Five hundred dollars each now and the rest later."

They were all ears. They wanted to have the two more days in Monaco and readily agreed to accompany them the short distance to Nice.

On the drive over, Doc couldn't help but think about why in the world the so-called Jenny with the light-brown hair had chosen to place her money in the bank in Nice rather than in Monaco or Switzerland. But it seemed she had, and that was that.

Once they arrived in Nice, Doc couldn't afford to take them to the bank in their bathing suits, so he took them to the nearest women's boutique and purchased them an outfit of their choice, along with shoes and hats.

They asked, "Why you get hats?"

"I'm not exactly sure, but maybe they will be a little more open with us since we are complete strangers, and we won't lose any time if they see you both dressed a little more conservatively."

When they showed them Roho's picture at the second financial establishment they visited, the man behind the counter was quick to make an identification and said that she had just been in with Madam Fox and two gentleman a day or two ago. He went on to say that Madam Fox had transferred some money and placed some jewelry into her safe deposit box.

Doc was overwhelmed with anxiety and thought, *Was Jenny Fox someone Swindle had double-crossed in the past, or what?*

When he recovered he asked, "Do you have any idea as to where their next destination might be? You know, this young lady is my granddaughter, and I need to locate her." He showed them Roho's picture again.

The bank teller gave him a peculiar look, and Doc immediately responded. "I know what you're thinking, but her daddy is from Colombia and she is part Hispanic."

"Oh, monsieur, let me think. When they left here I believe I overheard one of them say they were going to Marseille for a brief visit."

Dr. Suggs thanked him, and they hurriedly left the bank, having obtained the exact information they desired. He now knew that someone who went by the name of Jenny Fox had paid for the hit, but he couldn't make any connection to Swindle.

They then went to a sidewalk café, and Doc thanked the two young ladies from Barcelona for their help and asked if it would be terribly inconvenient if they paid them an additional five hundred dollars, plus cab fare back to Monaco. "Your help has been invaluable in my search for my granddaughter, and I thank you so very much. I need to let her know that her mother is extremely ill."

The women gladly took the money. Doc hailed a cab for the young women and wished them a safe trip back to Monaco and a pleasant vacation at the resort.

Eldridge couldn't restrain himself, and as soon as the young women had gotten in the cab, he had to ask. "Mr. Gibbs, how long have you been working with the boss, or are you the boss?"

"Like I said earlier, Eldridge, it's been a while. Can't you look at me and see how old I am?"

"Yes, sir, but that doesn't answer my question."

"I'm sorry, but that's the best I can do right now. I hope you'll understand."

Eldridge thought for a moment and realized that he probably shouldn't have asked.

Chapter 23

WHEN THEY LEFT FOR MARSEILLE, Eldridge could no longer restrain himself. He had to know why Mr. Gibbs was making the trip. "Mr. Gibbs, exactly why are we over here? So far, everyone has done what they were supposed to."

Without hesitating, Dr. Suggs lied, "Eldridge, that's exactly why we're here. We're following up to make sure everyone does exactly what they're supposed to do. You know that in any operation everything has to be carried out exactly as it should be. Thus far, they've made several mistakes."

The perplexed Eldridge commented, "How's that, Mr. Gibbs? I thought you said they were on schedule."

"They are, my good man, they're exactly on schedule. The only trouble is they are very easy to track. Did you think about that?"

Eldridge frowned and scratched his head. "No, not really. What difference does it make?"

"Quite a bit, Eldridge, quite a bit. You can never tell who is trying to get in the same business, if you know what I mean."

"Yeah, I guess so," the sullen Eldridge replied.

"Good, Eldridge, good. Now when we get to Marseille I'll betcha anything we'll be able to pick up their trail without any problem." Doc was not as confident as he sounded, but he needed to keep Eldridge alert and thinking that they were not alone.

It had the desired effect. Eldridge remained quiet for a while and finally asked, "Is the fact that they're easy to follow gonna be held against us?"

"No, my good friend," the bluffing Dr. Suggs answered with a certain amount of fake confidence. "We're just going to use what we find out to help clean up the operation. You know, this will be my last one."

Eldridge turned to him and asked, "Mr. Gibbs, are you really retiring?"

"Yes. I don't plan to spend the rest of my life meandering around all over the world, checking on things."

"I can't say I blame you. A man of your age oughta be able to sit back and enjoy life. You know, Mr. Gibbs, you ain't no spring chicken, and this work can be hard at times."

"You're right, son. I'm glad you understand. You know, I noticed the way you looked at those girls that we picked up in Monaco. I thought for a minute that you were going to try to make out with one of them, but that would have been a mistake, since all we needed from them was their help to find Roho and the others and see what they are up to."

This was exactly what Eldridge had had in his mind at the time, but after hearing what Doc said, he was not about to admit it.

Doc noticed his response and commented, "I'll tell you what, my man. All work and no play is not very good for anyone. Since we're a little bit ahead of the folks we're following, maybe when we get to Marseille you can find some young lady to your liking."

Eldridge could only wonder how this old man knew what he had in mind. "What makes you think, Mr. Gibbs, that I'm looking for a woman?"

"Eldridge, I was young once, and you seem to be a normal man in most every respect. I'd be surprised, after the way you looked at those two girls in Monaco, that you weren't looking for a young lady. You know, I probably would myself if I was about forty or fifty years younger, but that's in the past. I'm too old for things like that while on a job."

Eldridge was quick to ask, "How long you gonna gimme when we get to Marseille?"

"I thought I said a minute ago, Eldridge, a night on the town—that is, if you're careful. You know these folks don't particularly like strangers, and even if they did, it's a dangerous place."

Eldridge thought about what he said before speaking. "Yes, sir, you're right. It's gonna be hard to find two innocent-looking, clean, young women like the ones that accompanied us to Nice."

Doc didn't know how to answer him. He knew he was right, that the two peasant girls from Barcelona were indeed much more innocent than the ones they would run into in Marseille. In addition, he was a little taken back by Eldridge's remark of finding two women. Doc had just said that he was old, and here Eldridge was talking about two women in Marseille. Surely, Eldridge wasn't planning on going with two at one time, and therefore, that left him to surmise that he was planning on one for Doc. He thought, *Is he trying to compromise me?*

"Eldridge, son, you're smart beyond your years. However, I'll bet you'll be able to find a young woman to your liking in Marseille." Doc hoped that he had emphasized a singular woman for Eldridge, and not one for him. He wasn't about to mix work and play. Anyway, he couldn't cheat on the lovely Hooker County women.

"If you say so, Mr. Gibbs."

"That I do, son, that I do. Now watch your driving. It shouldn't be long before we get there."

Chapter 24

WHILE ELDRIDGE WAS SPENDING THE night with a young French woman, who said she was from Lyon, Doc was busily studying the map and trying to figure out the Bordeaux region and which route to take. There were really only two good routes to follow, but he couldn't help but wonder what they would do when they got to the Bordeaux region. That left a lot of open territory. Plus, he felt they weren't alone. He was reasonably sure they were being followed.

Finally, when he got tired of thinking, he fell asleep and slept until six o'clock the next morning. When he got up he took a sponge bath, shaved, and went to have breakfast. Much to his surprise, he ran into Eldridge and a relatively good-looking young woman in the dining room.

Before he had finished eating, a spastic Eldridge came over and introduced the young lady. "Mr. Gibbs, I would like for you to meet Mademoiselle Saint Marie from Lyon."

Doc introduced himself as Percy Gibbs and asked the young lady what she did in Lyon.

Without so much as a blink of an eyelid, she told him that she was a nun who taught in a local Catholic school. This was shocking to Doc, and after taking a sip of his strong French coffee, he said, "That's a fine vocation, young lady. We need more good teachers like you. Where did you learn your English?"

"Oh, at the Sorbonne, as well as while I was working as an au pair in Boston."

"It's a small world, isn't it, Eldridge? To think that you would run into such a lovely lady here in Marseille of all places, who is well versed and widely traveled."

Eldridge dropped his head and said, "Yes, sir, Mr. Gibbs."

With that, Doc stood, shook her hand, and said, "I'm sorry, Miss Saint Marie, but my friend and I are going to be leaving shortly. I do trust that you two have had a good evening together?"

She clung to Eldridge and asked if he couldn't stay another day. Eldridge looked at Doc, as if he wanted to ask.

For a moment Doc was about to grant her request in order to find out more about her, but then he decided that they needed to head on to Toulouse. She acted as though she was heartbroken, but it was fairly obvious to Doc that she was doing a good bit of acting.

"Miss Saint Marie," Doc said, rather than addressing her as Sister, "Why don't you give my friend here your address so he can look you up when we are in Lyon."

This got her attention. It was fairly obvious to Doc that for some reason she didn't want to be seen with either of them in Lyon. However, she did give Eldridge a phone number and told him she would be glad to meet him in Paris wherever, whenever.

Doc thought, *Wherever, whenever? Poor old Eldridge is going to be sorry he ran into her. I wonder who she is and where she's really from.*

Doc smiled and asked to be excused.

Chapter 25

THEY DIDN'T SPEAK MUCH ON the trip to Toulouse. Doc was preoccupied with whether or not they were being followed and how they were going to locate Roho and her group in the Bordeaux region. Eldridge was still hung over and thinking about the young lady from Lyon and wondering what Mr. Gibbs thought about what he had done. Would he hold this against him? He didn't know.

Finally, Eldridge got around to asking. "Mr. Gibbs, I didn't tell the young lady from Lyon anything. I hope you understand that."

"Aw, Eldridge, why should I care? Y'all will probably never see each other again. She'll go back to her job, if indeed she is a nun and teaches at a Catholic girl's school in Lyon, and you'll go on working for the outfit. The only thing that puzzles me about her is that she seemed to know a good bit about the good old USA and her English was perfect, except for a hint of a midwestern accent. In the future I would suggest that you limit your peccadilloes to one of the less sophisticated French women."

In order to shake up Eldridge a little more, he went ahead and said, "You know, she was looking to hook up with us, so to speak. You don't suppose she could be working for someone else, do you? Do you think she could be checking up on us? Something to think about, isn't it, Eldridge?"

By now, Eldridge was not only drowsy from lack of sleep, but shook up over what Doc was saying. He pulled the car over to the shoulder of the road, told Doc that he needed to relieve himself, and asked him if he wouldn't drive the rest of the way to Toulouse. "I'm tired and I ache all over."

Doc smiled at a shaky Eldridge and replied, "Sure, son. What's the matter? Did you have a tough night?"

"You can say that again. That woman showed me things I'd never seen or heard of before. Damn, I feel like I've been run over by a Mack truck. That woman and the cognac were tough."

"You reckon she learned that in the monastery, Eldridge?" Doc knew this comment would only add to Eldridge's turmoil concerning the woman who said she was a nun and taught in a Catholic girl's school.

"No, sir, I don't think so. She probably learned it, oh, I don't know where. Probably some older Frenchman in town taught her before she entered the convent. You know how they say the French do."

"No, I'm not sure I do, but that's a possibility."

Chapter 26

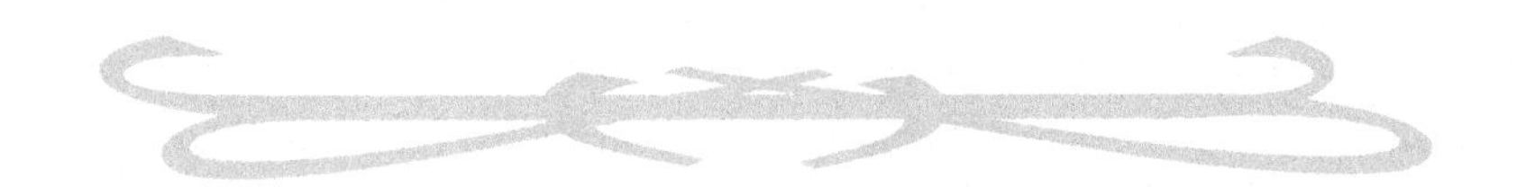

Doc had had an eerie feeling, ever since they left Nice, that they were being followed. One thing was for sure, Eldridge hadn't been the same since he had spent the night with the young woman who said she was from Lyon. He was sleeping and twitching from time to time.

The moment they arrived in downtown Toulouse, Dr. Suggs parked in front of a two-star hotel, woke up Eldridge, and told him that they needed to check in for the night. It was apparent to Doc that he needed to make some changes before they completed their journey. Eldridge didn't object, and when they got out of the car Doc deliberately left the key in the ignition. He opened the boot, got out his valise, and led Eldridge into the hotel, where they registered in two second-story rooms facing the street.

It was time for the evening meal, but when he went to get Eldridge he said he was too tired and shaky from the night before.

"If it's all right with you, Mr. Gibbs, I think I'll just go to sleep. I don't have much of an appetite. Damn, that cognac is some sorta tough stuff. I'm cramping all over for some reason."

Doc couldn't help but wonder what had happened to Eldridge. It surely couldn't have been his little dalliance the evening before. This prompted Dr. Suggs to leave the hotel, go to a nearby clothing store, and purchase a new outfit and a pair of dark sunglasses. He then went to an automobile agency that he had noted on the drive in and told one of the salesmen, who could speak very little English, that he needed to purchase a car that could make it through the Pyrenees in the event that he had to drive over to Spain.

The man got another salesman to help him understand English, and Doc bought a used Citroen. After showing the appropriate papers and paying about twice what the car was worth, they arranged to pick it up the next day.

When he reached the parked car, he placed the gift-wrapped package containing the dildo on the backseat of the Volkswagen, went to a restaurant, and had one of the worst meals he had ever eaten in his life. Not knowing French, he couldn't read anything on the menu. What he really wanted was a large juicy steak, a potato, and some Worcestershire sauce, but he was a little afraid to ask for steak because he had heard that some of the French loved to eat horse meat. The last time he had eaten horse meat was when he was in the service during the World War II.

When his meal arrived, he couldn't eat anything except the bread. He wondered who in the world would want to eat fresh pasta with black truffles and cream. He paid a veritable fortune for the meal, thanked the waiter, and went to his room.

Once in his room, he sat back from the window, where it would be hard for anyone to recognize him, and looked to see what would transpire next. Sure enough, the young man with whom he had negotiated at the car dealership to drive the Volkswagen to Bordeaux came and drove away. As to whether or not he was going to Bordeaux, Doc didn't know. At least he was going in the right direction, he hoped.

He waited until it was too dark to see if anyone would follow the Volkswagen. When he didn't notice anything suspicious, he decided to go to bed and get a good night's sleep. Sleep was elusive. He kept thinking, *Someway, somehow, someone knows where we are. I believe someone has put a global positioning device on the Volkswagen.* He fretted for a while, trying to figure out when and where it could have been placed on the Volkswagen. In his mind, it would have had to have been in Nice. Of course, it could have been some other place, but Nice seemed to be the most logical place. If one was on there, they would no doubt end up in Bordeaux across from the police station—that is, if they didn't stop the unsuspecting young man somewhere along the way who he had hired to drive the car. If not, they might try to follow him and Eldridge the next morning when they left in the Citroen.

Doc became so restless that he decided to go to the bathroom and take a shower. It was located at the end of the hall and didn't have a shower. It only had a commode, a sink, and a small cast-iron bathtub, which didn't look like it had been used in weeks. This was not to his liking, so he returned to his room, got his washbowl, and went back to the bathroom. He filled it with cold water, sponged off, and shaved like he had the previous night before going to bed.

When he got back in the bed, he still couldn't sleep. He kept thinking about the young woman who said she was from Lyon and had spent time in Boston. To him, her English sounded more like someone from the Midwest. There was one thing for sure, she certainly hadn't picked up her dialect at the Sorbonne or Boston. After mulling this over for a while, he wondered if the still-lethargic and spastic Eldridge knew her first name. All he knew was Mademoiselle Saint Marie, but what was her first name? It surely wasn't Saint, and he doubted if her name was Saint Marie. After fretting about this for a while, he got up and went into Eldridge's room to see if he had a global positioning device on him.

Eldridge didn't, unless it was in his cell phone. He needed to know for sure, so he removed the phone, went downstairs, found a truck that was en route to Paris, and placed it in the back.

With this accomplished, he returned to his room, fluffed his pillow, and went to sleep, wondering why she didn't say she was Sister Saint Marie when he had deliberately called her Miss.

Who in the heck was she? Was she after the money, or what?

Chapter 27

THE NEXT MORNING DOC FOUND himself humming "Fool on the Hill" by Herb Alpert and Sergio Mendes. It wasn't that he liked bossa nova that much; he was trying to put two and two together. If he had had his preference, he would have loved some jazz from the Hot Club in Paris, which was recorded during the 1930s. He was thinking about Marta Roho, who, according to Swindle, was humming something that sounded like "The Girl from Ipanema" while she put her clothes on and left his room, thinking Swindle was dying.

Doc tried to wipe that out of his mind by thinking, *I wonder why I thought that. Exactly what is wrong with Eldridge? He is acting just like someone I remember from my childhood who drank Jamaica ginger, as they called it. Looks kinda like he's got the jake leg. Had to have gotten hold of some bad cognac.*

He suddenly decided to go to the bathroom, fill up his washbowl, return to his room, wash his face, and put on the clothing he had bought the evening before. After dressing, he went next door to wake up Eldridge.

Doc couldn't help but think that somewhere along the way he had done something foolish by not asking for a description of Jenny Fox and the men when they were in the bank. Too late now. That was in the past, and they needed to move on. He only hoped that whoever was following them would be foolish enough to follow the Volkswagen to Bordeaux or the truck with Eldridge's cell phone in it to Paris.

He found Eldridge sweaty and still suffering from the aftereffects of his evening in Marseille. When he finally got him awake, he noticed that he was having muscle spasms and surmised that he was having difficulty focusing.

Once up, Eldridge started down the hall to the bathroom to take a bath. Doc wished him good luck.

"What'd you say, Mr. Gibbs?"

"Good luck, son. You know the tub is very small and there's no hot water. You know we're not staying at the Ritz. This hotel is a two-star and is very old. It kinda reminds me of when I was growing up." He was lying, of course. He'd never stayed in a place like this before but thought his reason for doing so was good. The only thing he knew for sure was that Eldridge was walking with a slightly spastic gait and didn't quite seem to be himself.

When Eldridge returned he looked like he was in a state of shock. Doc could tell that something had gotten him upset, so he asked, "What's troubling you? What's happened?"

"Man, that's the nastiest place I've ever been in. I bet that tub hadn't been cleaned out in a week."

"There's more than one way to skin a cat. What did you do?" Doc asked, observing a spastic Eldridge.

"Mr. Gibbs, I hope I didn't get anyone wet on the floor below, but I turned on the cold water in the tub and stood outside and rinsed off real good."

"Good, excellent idea. I wish I'd thought of it. Now hurry up because we need to leave, and I'll drive if it's all right with you. You still seem tired from your evening with the girl from Lyon."

Eldridge knew there was something wrong with him and surmised that most of it had been secondary to the fact that they had drunk a good bit of cognac in Marseille. "That's fine with me. Do you know the way to Bordeaux?"

"No, not really, but I've got a map. We shouldn't have any trouble getting there. Since we're running a little behind time, why don't we pass up eating breakfast here and wait until we get to one of the bed-and-breakfasts down the road? You know, I've always wanted to eat at an inn in France, and at my age I doubt I'll ever come back to France again."

"Okay, Mr. Gibbs, but I'm hungry enough to eat the whole hog. You know I haven't had any solid food in my stomach in over twenty-four hours."

"Eldridge, I don't believe we'll find a whole hog, but I bet we can find something a little better than what was on the menu here last night. You know, they almost cleaned me out, selling me pasta and black truffles."

"Black truffles and pasta?"

"Yeah."

"Why'd you order that, Mr. Gibbs?"

"I can't read French, and the waiter refused to take my order in English. You know how it is in certain parts of France, don't you?"

"No, not really."

"For your information, some of the French think it's the only language in the world, and if you can't speak it, they won't wait on you. They think Americans are crude and stupid."

"Oh."

"Yep, that's right, son. Now hurry up and let's go."

When they walked outside, for the first time Eldridge noticed the outfit Doc had on and asked, "Where'd you get that, Mr. Gibbs?"

"Oh, I picked it up. You know the old saying, 'When in Rome do as the Romans do.' I figured while we're in France, I'd just dress like a fella from the south of France."

When they approached the place where they had parked the previous night, Eldridge exclaimed, "Damn, you know our car's gone!"

"Whatta you mean, Eldridge, our car's gone?"

"It's not in the parking lot, and it's not on the street anywhere that I can see."

"My goodness, I guess we'll have to go to a place I spotted last night when I was out trying to find a hamburger and see if we can't get another set of wheels."

"Yes, sir, but I sure would like to get my hands on the bastards that stole the Volkswagen."

"Oh, that's all right, son. That thing was about worn out, and anyway, we might have to do a little mountain climbing along the way. Yeah, we might even end up in Spain somewhere."

By now, Eldridge was beginning to think that the old man had really lost his wits and asked, "What the hell for?"

"Oh, Muhammed might have taken the women there, particularly the one with the money. You like money, don't you, son?"

With that, Doc started back to humming "Fool on the Hill" and started walking, taking his usual short, choppy steps, toward the car dealership.

Eldridge didn't say anything. He just slowed down and followed.

Doc broke the silence by asking, "You like Sergio Mendes and Brasil '66?"

"Not particularly. I'm trying to figure out why you think they might be in Spain."

Doc didn't answer Eldridge right away. He just kept on talking about music to see what his reaction was. "It's pretty good music. I bet you'd like 'Sunrise.'"

"Naw, can't say that I do."

"How about a little Chicago Blues, like maybe some Buddy Guy?"

"He's all right."

"Eldridge, being from the South, I like most all the blues, you know. Have you ever heard Robert Johnson?"

"No, sir." *What's this old man up to?*

"He was mighty good until he drank some whiskey with strychnine in it. It killed him before he was thirty years old."

"If you say so, Mr. Gibbs. Why in the hell are you bringing all this music stuff up?"

"Heck, son, I don't know. Could be because you've been stiff as a poker ever since we left Marseille. You know, after your evening with the girl from Lyon."

This got Eldridge's attention, and he replied, "Whatta you think, she put some strychnine in my cognac?"

"No, not at all, but for some reason you're mighty stiff. Now close your left eye, look at the sign down the street, and read it for me."

Eldridge couldn't read it.

"Now close your right eye and see if you can read it."

He still couldn't read the sign.

"Now, can you read it with both eyes open?"

His vision was fuzzy, and Eldridge answered, "No, sir."

"I don't know about the cognac, but that, or some of the food you had, has certainly brought about a change in you. Of course, I don't think you need to worry because you're better than you were this time last night. It'll likely wear off. There's nothing to worry about. I'm sure that lovely nun wouldn't have spiked your drink or food."

Eldridge stopped and looked at Doc. "Mr. Gibbs, do you think that two-timing bitch, whoever she is, coulda caused me to feel the way I do?"

"I don't know, son, but it'll wear off and you'll be fine."

"How do you know?"

"Eldridge, I just know. You're a lot better than you were yesterday, and I'm sure if you think about it you'll agree."

"Well, yes, sir, I guess so. I really didn't think about it at the time. I just thought we'd tied a good one on."

"I didn't think about it much myself, son, I just thought that y'all had really had a big night until I noticed how spastic you were. Now come on and let's make our way to the automobile dealership. You're a big man, and whatever it was wasn't enough to do you in."

When they arrived at the automobile dealership, he located the Frenchman with whom he had dealt the evening before and asked him about the Citroen. He was told it was gassed and ready to go.

"Good, monsieur. Would you mind putting it on the grease rack and letting me check underneath it first?"

Eldridge knew for sure that Doc wasn't being honest with him and asked, "What did you do with the Volkswagen? Don't you trust me? What's up, man?"

Doc looked up at him and pointedly said, "To a point, son, to a point."

"That means that you don't trust me, Mr. Gibbs."

"No, son," he lied. "In this business you can only trust people so far. You oughta know that if you are going to live to be as old as I am. Now as to the Volkswagen, someone drove it off last night."

"Why didn't you call me, Mr. Gibbs? I'd a shot the bastard."

"Oh, son, it wasn't worth it. Anyway, it would have attracted undue attention, and we don't need that. You realize we're here on false papers and we've got to find the girls and get the money. Right?"

"Why didn't you tell me, Mr. Gibbs?" a suspicious Eldridge asked again.

"I'm sorry, Eldridge, I guess it's because I'm used to working alone," he lied.

The salesman was preoccupied with the fact that he thought that Doc didn't trust him, and he wondered why Doc was questioning whether or not he had checked it over and had it ready to go.

Doc tried as best he could, due to the language barrier, to explain to the Frenchman that he was looking for a global positioning device of some sort. After two or three other Frenchmen came forward and he finally got across to them what he was looking for, they put it up on the grease rack and Doc and Eldridge checked everything that looked suspicious. When they couldn't find anything, Doc paid the Frenchman another ten euros, shook his hand, and thanked him. He and Eldridge got in the car and left.

When they turned south rather than north, Eldridge asked, "Mr. Gibbs, have you missed the road?"

"No, I don't think so, son. I thought we'd just go this way. While we're here, we might as well enjoy the view. There should be a bed-and-breakfast up the road, and if not, we can stop in Lourdes."

Eldridge didn't like the idea of Doc not trusting him but went along with him, since he thought he was in charge of the whole operation. He knew Doc probably thought the girl from Lyon had spiked his drink. With that, he again asked, "Mr. Gibbs, are you sure I'm gonna be all right?"

"Yes, son, I'm pretty sure. In fact, I'm almost certain that you're going to be all right. Now, let's pull in at this inn and get something to eat."

When they got out of the car, Doc looked around and asked Eldridge if he saw any evidence that anyone was following them.

Eldridge looked but couldn't help but wonder why Doc was still preoccupied with being following, but he let it go and they went inside and ordered breakfast.

Doc had them fix him six eggs over well, a loaf of French bread, and a cup of coffee.

The French family didn't know quite what to think, but when he offered them enough money they didn't bother to think anymore. They went ahead and fixed what he ordered. Eldridge ordered two croissants with ham and cheese in them and a cup of coffee.

When they finished their meal and went outside, Doc looked around again and there was no one in sight. Not seeing anyone didn't mean a thing. He was still suspicious and asked, "Eldridge, do you think you can see well enough to drive this thing? If so, let's get on with it and head toward Biarritz. It's easier to start at the bottom and work your way up. Anyway, we've got a little extra time on our hands, and I'm sure you'll enjoy the beaches."

"What beaches?"

"Aw, Eldridge, it used to be a famous vacation spot frequented by members of the European aristocracy up to and including Napoleon III and his Spanish princess Eugenie, Queen Victoria of England, and other members of the royal family."

"Well, what happened to it?" Eldridge asked, thinking that Doc was still leading him on.

"Nothing much. It just became commercialized, and the rich and famous moved on to other places. However, as I understand, it's still a pretty nice place. You don't mind taking a detour, do you, Eldridge? Anyway, you need to get over what happened to you in Marseille."

Eldridge wasn't in a very good mood, thinking about how he had been tricked by the woman from Lyon and the fact that Doc wasn't leveling with him, but he went ahead and did as he was told. After all, he had accompanied the old man by train from Chicago to New Orleans and by boat to England and by car to the south of France.

They remained quiet for a while before Doc finally asked, "What was that good-looking nun from Lyon's first name? I'm sure you've told me, but I've forgotten."

Eldridge gave him a blank stare and replied, "You know, I don't believe she told me, and I forgot to ask. Damn, I've been a fool!"

"Where's the address she gave you? Maybe she wrote her first name down on it."

Eldridge looked in his pocket and couldn't find the envelope on which she had written the address. He couldn't find it because Doc had removed it and placed it with the gift in the backseat of the Volkswagen the night before.

Doc noticed how disturbed Eldridge was, searching through his pockets for the envelope with the address on it, and said, "My goodness, Eldridge, I wish you hadn't lost it. How are you going to know how to get in touch with her when you recover from the other night?"

Eldridge became angry. "Hell, Mr. Gibbs, stop playing games with me. Exactly what are you up to? You know that woman don't plan on seeing me again after what she tried to do to me."

Chapter 28

Doc, still preoccupied with the thought that someone knew exactly where they were, answered, "I'm not playing games with you. I'm playing a game with who's trying to follow us. I'm a fair judge of character, and I believe I can trust you. It appears to me that we're in the wrong business. In fact, that's why I'm getting out after this particular gig, as you call it, is over. Now you keep your eyes on the road, and I'll look. If you ask me, that girl from Lyon could be working for the fella that sent you with me. Then again, there's no telling who she's working for. In any event, I have no idea why she would follow us unless she's after the same thing we are."

"What's that, Mr. Gibbs?"

"Money, son, money. Finding the money."

All the time Doc was thinking, *If you wallow with hogs, you end up smelling like them, if not acting like them, and if I ever get out of this mess, I'll never get back in anything like it again.*

Doc saw Eldridge scratching and asked, "You didn't notice any blood on you or on the sheets this morning, did you?"

Puzzled by what Doc asked, Eldridge asked, "No, why?" *Is this old man still playing around with me, or is he really getting senile? I know he's in charge, and maybe that's the reason I'm here to look after him, since this is his last big gig.*

"Bedbugs, son, bedbugs."

"Mr. Gibbs, whatta you talking about?" Eldridge nervously asked.

"Oh, I forgot. You're too young to know about bedbugs. They are insects that are making a comeback since we've quit using DDT and other pesticides.

They don't carry any specific disease that I'm aware of. I found some bedbugs in my bed last night, and I'm wondering if that is why you're scratching."

Eldridge pulled the car over to the side of the road and stopped. He pulled up his shirt and asked, "I don't see any, do you, Mr. Gibbs?"

Doc put on his glasses and examined Eldridge's torso. "I don't see any blood, but I see where you could have had some bites. But don't worry about it. Like I said, they don't carry any specific disease that I'm aware of. Although, it might be a good idea when we get to Lourdes to rent a room, take a good shower, and buy you some new clothes, since it might get cool at night up in the Pyrenees—that is, if we have to go to Spain."

Doc now felt sure that he could trust Eldridge and told him that they had to be extremely cautious from now on, since it seemed likely to him that a lot of people were interested in what they were doing.

"How so?" Eldridge asked.

"Like I said earlier, money, son, money. Someone knows that we are trying to locate the woman who has the money and find out what happened to her. You know money's the root of all evil, don't you?"

"No, sir. It sure can buy you a lotta good things."

"That's correct, but it can also buy you a lot of trouble. I think we're going to run into a lot of trouble before this is over. Now get the car back on the road and let's head to Lourdes."

When they got to Lourdes, Doc had Eldridge pull up to a hotel, and he rented a room so Eldridge could take a good bath. While he was inside, Doc pulled the car around the block and watched the entrance to the hotel.

Sure enough, shortly after he left the entrance to the hotel and pulled around the block, a Renault with two young men with dark complexions pulled up to the curb about a half block away from the hotel and parked.

When Eldridge finished showering and changing clothes, he threw his old clothes away. He didn't know what a bedbug was, but he was afraid some might be in them. When he came out of the hotel and couldn't locate Doc, his first thought was that the old man had ditched him. But why?

When Doc saw him looking lost and bewildered, he got out of the Citroen, walked in the opposite direction from the Renault around the block, and when he got close enough to whistle, he did. This got Eldridge's attention, and he noticed Doc motioning for him to follow him.

Eldridge thought, *What the hell? I might as well. This old man may be smarter than I think he is, and anyway he's too small to cause any trouble, since he hasn't got his suitcase full of guns with him.*

When Eldridge reached Doc he told him not to look back and to just keep following him. "There are two men sitting in a Renault parked about a half block from the hotel, and I have a suspicion they are following us."

"You don't think they have anything to do with the woman from Lyon, do you?"

"I have no idea, Eldridge. All I know is that they are following us. It could be that she's in Bordeaux or else in Paris."

"How so, Mr. Gibbs?"

"I'll explain to you later, but right now let's go get in the car and head for Biarritz. Of course, somewhere along the way we'll probably need to delay them temporarily."

"Delay them temporarily—what do you mean, Mr. Gibbs?"

"Aw, son, don't ask too many questions. Look at the map when we get to this spot. Over the rise there is a hairpin turn. I believe that's where we'll stop them."

"Stop them?"

"Yes, son, stop them."

"Okay, if you say so, Mr. Gibbs," Eldridge, still twitching a little, said in a rather subdued voice. After all, he was tired of following the old man around, and he had been right on every occasion so far. The only thing he couldn't explain was why he went by train to New Orleans and boat to England and bought a car and went by ferry to France in the old Volkswagen. He had trouble understanding why he had let someone take the Volkswagen, but he wasn't about to ask.

When they reached the rise that Doc had pointed out to him on the map, Eldridge asked, "Is this it, Mr. Gibbs?"

"Yes, I believe so. I'll tell you what. I'm going to get my valise from the backseat, and as soon as we get over the top I want you to let me out and you stop just after you make the hairpin turn. Okay?"

"Okay, if you say so, Mr. Gibbs."

Doc reached in the back, opened the valise, pulled out the sniper rifle he had purchased in New Orleans, and started to assemble it.

This scared Eldridge, and he said, "Mr. Gibbs, what are you gonna do with that thing? I didn't know you had that with you. You know, we coulda gotten picked up with all that heat there."

"Aw, son, look. You've got an Uzi under your coat and that nine-millimeter Glock in your belt, and no one has stopped you. Why do you think we went by boat to England? It wasn't just for the ride! We had to take some extra things with us that we couldn't get on a plane with. Do you understand? Of course, I am scared of flying."

"Yes, sir. You're not gonna kill 'em, are you?" Eldridge nervously asked.

"No, I'm just going to delay them temporarily. You know, out here on this back road they could be hung up for a day or two. That is, if I can make it back to where you'll be parked. Of course, I've got to make two clean shots. As a rule, you know," Doc said as if he were an expert, "that's about all a sniper can get off without being located. In fact, sometimes you can only get off one, but I need to get off two," he said as he screwed the silencer on after he assembled the rifle.

Eldridge kept staring at him, and Doc cautioned him to keep his eye on the road and not worry about the gun because he didn't have any ammunition in it. He was only going to take two cartridges with him, since that was all he would need.

When they got over the top of the hill, Eldridge stopped long enough to let Doc out.

Doc, with his bad ankle, made it up the hill to where he had an open view of a car when it got within a couple hundred yards of him. They had arrived a little quicker than he had expected in the Renault, and he didn't have time to compensate for the wind or anything else. It worked out to where it wouldn't be necessary, since it would be a shot almost straight on.

He planned to make the first one hit the right front wheel and blow out the tire, and if there was no one in the backseat, he was going to shoot a hole through the rear tire and maybe the gas tank. The only thing was that he wasn't sure where the gas tank was on a Renault, since he hadn't seen one in quite some time.

Doc had trouble propping the heavy rifle on a limb and fired the first shot right through the right front tire, causing the car to swerve to the right. This interfered with his second shot, but by the time he loaded again and shot, they had stopped. This was the perfect shot; the second one went directly through the right rear tire and oddly enough hit something causing it to catch on fire but not explode.

Doc was relieved that it didn't explode, and eased his way over the edge of the hill down to where Eldridge was waiting. He got back in the Citroen, disassembled his rifle, and placed it on the backseat as they eased down the hill before restarting the engine.

"You didn't kill 'em, did you, Mr. Gibbs?" Eldridge asked with his voice trembling.

"No, I just shot out the right front tire and the right rear tire, and it caught on fire. They got out of there and took off running in the opposite direction."

"Why'd they do that?"

"Because the second shot caused it to catch on fire. It didn't explode, but apparently they were afraid it might and took off running."

"Well, who are they?" Eldridge asked.

"I think I know, but I don't know for sure. So for right now I'll just say I don't know. Anyway, forget about 'em. This is going to give us another twenty-four hours. We might even have time to enjoy the beach in Biarritz."

Chapter 29

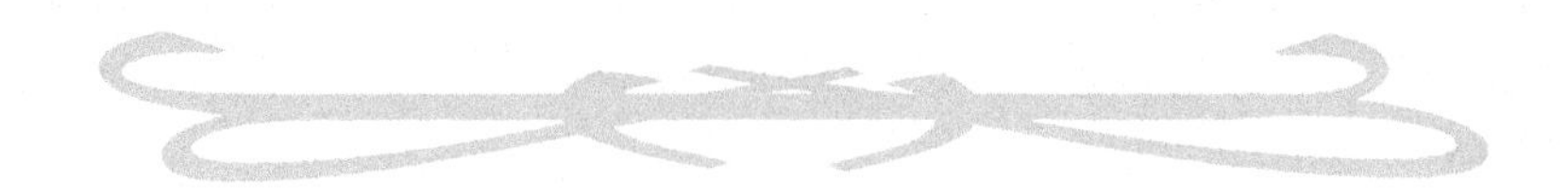

As soon as they arrived in Biarritz, Doc told Eldridge that they needed to see if they could find some Muslim brothers and goats.

This was a shock to Eldridge. "Why Muslim brothers and goats, Mr. Gibbs?"

"My goodness, Eldridge, don't you remember what we said to the so-called girl from Ipanema when we paid the visit to her hotel room? Muhammed made it up, and we went along with him and the woman he called Dummy. I'm sure he didn't go to the trouble of taking either woman to Africa or the Middle East. He just took the money and got rid of them in Southern France or Spain."

"What makes you say that, Mr. Gibbs?"

"Two and two makes four, Eldridge."

"How so?"

"Muhammed may be a fine man, but he's not like us. He's apparently spent quite a bit of time in this region, so we'll look for goats. If he hasn't killed them, some Arab will have them pregnant and barefoot before long. The only question is who were the two men who went in the bank with them?"

Eldridge was now sure that the old man was not getting senile and he knew exactly what he was doing. He said, "Mr. Gibbs, I've got a confession to make."

This took Doc by surprise, and he said in a rather inquisitive manner, "How's that, son? You haven't been working for the other side or anything like that, have you?"

"Oh, no, sir. I just thought we were off on one of them crazy deals, since this was going to be your last gig, and that you might be one of them guys whose bread wadn't quite done."

"Bread not quite done?" This statement confused Doc, who had never heard the expression before.

"Yeah, you know what I mean. That's what they say about folks that are not quite all there."

"Truth is, I'm probably not quite all there, but I'm not completely out of the game yet, and as soon as we get this mess sorted out, I'm absolutely going to be out of the game for good. And I believe you should too. I just don't think you're cut out for this kind of action. I don't know you, but I have the distinct impression that you aren't really from Chicago. I believe that you're from someplace in the South. You know, you sound a little bit like you're from Georgia."

"How do you know that?"

"I'm not sure, but from the way you talk and the way you used to walk before whatever it was that you drank or ate, you sure remind me of a good old Georgia boy. I hope you don't take me calling you 'boy' wrong."

"No, sir, I guess not."

"Good, Eldridge, good, because I wouldn't want you to think that about me. I'm just an old man trying to make it through the rest of my life without getting knocked down, drugged out, or stepping in the wrong hole, if you know what I mean."

"No, sir," he emphatically said, "but I'm with you all the way."

"Eldridge, sounds like you want to spend a little time on the beach while we check around and see if we can find any Arabs and goats."

Eldridge sheepishly said, "I'd like that, Mr. Gibbs, but first I need to make a confession."

"Confess to what, son? I thought you confessed a minute ago as to what you thought about me and what you thought about the trip."

"No, that wasn't what I was fixing to say. I must confess that you are a lot sharper in your own way than most all of the other folks I've worked for since I've been in this business."

"I guess I should thank you, son. Now come on and let's go to the beach and get us some swimwear, or at least get you some. I don't think I'd look very good in any with my little old skinny legs and my gut hanging out. We need to see if we can't find out a little something about where our good friend

Muhammed might be. Do you reckon we can trust him? Do you know him, Eldridge?"

"Not at all. In fact, when I met him at the hotel, it was the first time I'd ever seen him. I just know he works for the same outfit."

"Good, good. If he works for the same outfit then he's not likely to cross us, I hope."

"Whatta you mean, you hope?" Eldridge asked, knowing full well that the group he worked for owed their allegiance to no one. They just enjoyed doing what they did.

Chapter 30

THE BEACH WAS COVERED WITH tourists from France, England, Spain, and Germany. It was a rather cosmopolitan group of middle-class people who were on a cheap weekend in the south of France.

They tried to act like tourists until they got hungry and stopped at a sidewalk café, where they took a table next to four Muslim men who were drinking coffee and chatting with each other.

Doc spread out a map of the region and asked Eldridge if he remembered where Muhammed might be.

"No, all I know is it's in this region."

Before Doc could say anything else, the waitress came over to take their order. Doc, not understanding French, asked one of the Arabs if he spoke French. He was in luck. One of the young men not only spoke fluent French, but good English, and helped them order. They ordered zucchini crepes, some sort of chicken in vinegar, and coffee.

While waiting for their meal, Doc and Eldridge returned to studying the map like they were trying to locate Muhammed.

When the Arabs finished their coffee and got up to leave, Doc told them they were trying to locate a young man who had been a student at the University of Chicago named Muhammed Erian, who lived close by on a goat farm.

The Arabs looked at each other as if they were puzzled. Then one of them spoke. "We have never heard of anyone by that name. No one raises goats around here."

One of the young men looked at the map and said, "The only goat herd I know about is in this region here," pointing to a remote region on the border between Spain and France.

Doc thanked them, and they left, talking rapidly in Arabic.

When they finished eating, Doc looked at his watch, turned to Eldridge, and said, "Son, I think it's time for us to leave. What do you say?"

"I believe you're right."

They took their map with the spot Doc had marked on it and headed farther into the Pyrenees.

No sooner had they left than Eldridge thought he spotted a car following them. They pulled off the road into a wooded area, stopped the car, and waited. While waiting, Eldridge took out his Uzi and checked his clip. It was empty. He then took his nine-millimeter Glock and checked it; it was empty also. When he noticed this, he said, "Damn, Mr. Gibbs, that woman from Lyon not only tried to kill me, she's disarmed me and stole my cell phone!"

"Disarmed you?" This statement by Eldridge was somewhat alarming to Doc, since he knew Eldridge had no extra ammunition.

"Yes, she took my ammunition. All we got left is your rifle."

"Maybe not, son, maybe not. Reach back in my valise and pull out that hog leg of mine."

Eldridge opened the valise, and in addition to the sniper rifle and two boxes of ammunition, there was a .44 Magnum with a nine-inch barrel on it. When he saw it, his eyes got as large as golf balls.

"Damn, you mean to say you shot this thing, Mr. Gibbs?"

"No, son, no, I've never shot it, and that's the God's truth. I just had it in case I needed it."

"Hell, it might be that we're gonna need it, Mr. Gibbs, particularly if those two duds pull off in this direction. I'm gonna shoot first and ask later," Eldridge nervously said.

Doc reached over, grabbed his arm, and said, "Oh no, don't do that. We don't want to hurt anyone. All we want to do is get this trip behind us. Let's hope it doesn't come to that. Now take that thing and stuff it in your pants and get a box of cartridges and put them in your pocket."

Eldridge did as he was told, and they waited and waited. Finally, the car they thought was following them slowly drove by on up the mountain.

Doc felt relieved, as did Eldridge, and said, "Son, if you can find a place to turn this thing around, let's ease back and get on the highway and follow them for a while. That is, unless they are just some innocent people. Anyway, we'll follow them. How does that sound?"

"If you say so, Mr. Gibbs," Eldridge reluctantly said.

They slowly followed, barely keeping the car in front of them in sight until it made a right turn.

Eldridge looked over at Doc and asked, "What do we do now?"

Doc, not knowing what to do, hastily said, "Straight ahead, straight ahead."

Chapter 31

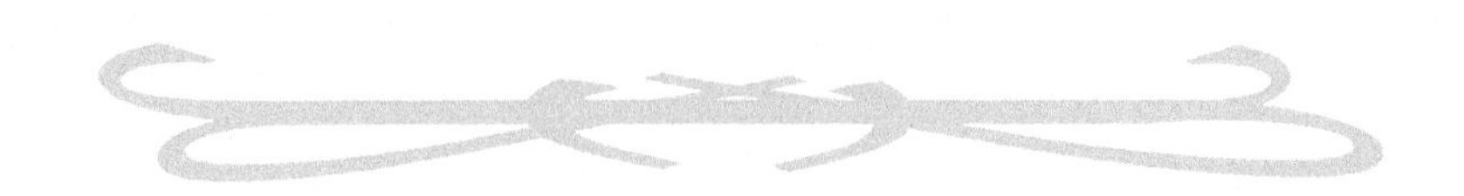

Doc looked over at Eldridge and said, with his amplified voice quivering, "I made a mistake when I told you to drive straight ahead."

Eldridge snapped his head around and asked, "How's that, Mr. Gibbs?"

"The Peugeot that turned off to the right a minute ago is now behind us."

"Damn!" Eldridge shouted in his deep baritone voice.

"Yeah, it looks like I've made a whopper of a mistake. It looks like the same people who've been following us since we left Toulouse."

"Why didn't you tell me?"

"I did. Don't you remember I told you they looked familiar when I shot the Renault?"

"Right. Whatta we gonna do, shoot 'em?"

"No, I hope it won't come to that, Eldridge."

"Why? Nobody'll find 'em for a few days if we drive their car off the road and let it drop into one of these ravines."

"Probably won't, but I don't want any blood on our hands, if it can be avoided. Do you?"

"No, sir, if we can help it. But if it comes down to us or them, it's gonna be them."

Doc was now as frightened as he had ever been in his life. "I wonder what they want with us, unless they're after the money too. Of course, they could be tied in with your friend from Lyon or maybe the law."

"How's that?"

Doc turned, reached over the seat, opened his valise, took out the scope, and tried to make out if they were the same people.

"Dang, Eldridge, it's the same ones, and like I said, there's something vaguely familiar about them. It could be that I've seen them before."

"How so? You probably have if they're the ones whose car you shot up. You wanna pull off the road and shoot their car again?"

"No; not yet, anyway."

"Whatta you mean?" Eldridge snapped.

"Aw, Eldridge, get ahold of yourself. You can't be half as scared as I am. Now, let's calm down and see if we can work this out some other way."

"I'm not scared, Mr. Gibbs."

"I'm glad you're not, but I'm so scared I'm about to crap in my pants. You know, it pays to be scared at times like this; it will help keep you alert—that is, if you don't panic."

"I'm not about to panic, if I can help it."

"Good. How do you think I got to be this old? I'll tell you, Eldridge, by being scared and thinking in situations like this. Now get over being upset and do not panic."

"What the hell do you propose we do, Mr. Gibbs?"

Doc noticed Eldridge's brown knuckles were almost pink from squeezing the steering wheel and tried to calm him. "My goodness, we've almost got them where we want them."

"What in the hell do you mean? It looks to me like they've got us."

"No, just think about it, Eldridge. We know exactly where they are, and unless they have a rocket launcher, we have the fire power. Can you throw a grenade?"

"A grenade? Why?" Eldridge anxiously shouted.

"I've got four in my valise. If they give us any trouble before we get to where we're going, we might have to disassemble their car and maybe them—that is, if you can throw a grenade that far. I know I can't. I probably wouldn't throw one far enough to where it would keep from blowing up our car. Yep, they might be behind us, but all the firepower is with us unless they've got some heat, as you call it, that I'm not aware of. To put it mildly, they are in a heap of trouble, Eldridge."

The calm way that the frightened Dr. Suggs said it relaxed Eldridge to some extent, and he asked, "When did you get them grenades?"

"On the boat on our way over from New Orleans to England."

"What?" Eldridge shouted.

"Yep, the Chinese on the boat were arms smugglers. Cost me an arm and a leg, so to speak. Didn't you know what they were carrying on the ship? I guess not, though, because I didn't until I talked to them about my time in China. Before I got my hands on the grenades, I was afraid we were going to wake up in the water without a boat or paddle wrapped in chains."

"Damn! Do you mean to say that we were on a boat full of ammunition with a bunch of smugglers?"

"Oh yeah. They were just a bunch of Chinese trying to make a living selling weapons to the highest bidder," he lied and added, "If I'd had any idea that you didn't suspect that, I would have told you."

Eldridge didn't answer. He just gawked at Doc and thought, *This feeble little old fella is bound to be the number-one dog in the outfit.*

While he had Eldridge confused, Doc felt like it was a good time to tell Eldridge about the money he had stashed away in the safe deposit box in New Orleans and who he thought was following them.

"Before we go any further, I feel that I should tell you a few things. I'm going to give you all the money in the other safe deposit box when we get back to New Orleans. Yep, that's exactly what I'm going to do, if we make it back. I'm ashamed to tell you, but before we left I wasn't sure I could trust you, and so I rented more than one box. In the one that you know about is where I put our papers and stuff. The money is in another one, which means if I don't get back, no one will get the money."

When he said that, he glanced over at Eldridge to see if this was soaking in. "I surely hope we get back for my sake, as well as yours. I need to die of old age, and you do too. My advice to you, Eldridge, is to get out of this line of work and take the money and invest it. It would probably be a good idea when you're ready to settle down that you find some nice young woman and get hitched up with her. Do you realize that, if the so-called nun from Lyon had had enough sense to correctly calculate the dosage of what she gave you, I might be attending your funeral? But don't worry, because it's behind us and you're gonna be all right. I guess she didn't take into account that you weighed almost three hundred pounds and was hard as a rock."

Doc shook his head in disgust and continued. "If she had been as good trying to get rid of people as she was sexually, she'd have probably done it. If we run into her again, I might suggest that she get a job working in a bordello in Paris rather than trying to carry out a hit, if that's the best she can do."

Eldridge started to say something, but Doc asked him to refrain until he had finished.

"One more thing, Eldridge, and then I'll be quiet for a while. I think I know, like I said, who those two lads following us are. They're probably Sancho and Ramon, or whoever the Hispanic guys are we met in the hotel in Chicago. I guess they have their eyes on the money too. Dang, if that's the case, we're all acting like a bunch of old hounds after a bitch in heat. Money makes people do all sorts of things."

"Yeah, I guess you could say that money, to some extent, is the root of all evil. Of course, there are other things that motivate people, like hate, fear, love, and, last but not least, things like winning at all cost. Of course, however you look at it, sooner or later we all end up the same way—dead. That's one rap you can't beat. At times we can postpone it, but we can't beat it."

Eldridge was having a hard time figuring out why the old man was rambling and why he wasn't making a move to do something about the people who were following them.

"Mr. Gibbs, if you're through, can I ask you another question?"

"Yep, sure can. What is it?"

"What do you propose to do?"

"Hmm, that's interesting. We've got several options. One is, like I mentioned earlier, we could do what you wanted to do. We could have a shoot-out with them or throw a grenade. Of course, that way we wouldn't really know what they were up to; we'd just know they wouldn't be following us anymore. Another option is we could stop and motion for them to catch up with us and ask them, but I'm not sure I want to do that right now. I think we oughta try a couple of other options first. We could pull off the road at the next house we see and wait and see what happens. The only thing wrong with that is they are bound to connect up with us again, and we won't really know what they're up to. Another good option is to let 'em follow us and see if they're really after the money, which they probably are. The way to prove that is to let them follow us until we locate Muhammed, if indeed we're in the right neighborhood, so to speak, and then we can have it out—hopefully in a civil way, like splitting up the money. I'm gonna give you my part because, as I said earlier, I don't want any of the money that I left in New Orleans. And I don't need any cut of the money that Muhammed and his group took from the person who hired the so-called girl from Ipanema to dispense with the attorney. Anyway, they may not know about the two men that went in the bank with the women to get the money. That will mean that maybe we can get them on our side if push comes to shove. Whatta you think?"

"Hell, I don't know, Mr. Gibbs. All I know is that we're in a tough spot."

"You're right about that, Eldridge, you're right about that. It doesn't get a lot tougher than this, or at least it won't until we catch up with Muhammed. You know Muhammed wasn't supposed to kill the woman, and he was supposed to send half of the money back to the guy that told y'all to meet me in the hotel. That means we've just got half of the money to split up. That'll be between Muhammed, the two Hispanics behind us, you, and maybe the two men who went into the bank with the women. Lord only knows what's happened to your friend from Lyon and how she figures in this. It could be that she and the two men who took the women to the bank are working on their own. What do you think?"

"I'm not sure, and I'm not sure I really want to know."

"Me neither, Eldridge. I just want to get this over with so I can retire and get back to the simple life. You know, the simple life is a lot more fun than the one we're living right now. I don't believe I could stand any more of this, so I sure hope we can get something worked out. Now let's drive on and act like there's no one behind us. I sure wish I knew exactly who the girl from Lyon is and her part in this operation. If I had to guess, and that's exactly what I'm doing, she might know the two other men. You don't reckon she's working for the same outfit that we are, do you?"

"I don't know, but you're supposed to. You're in charge."

"I'm only in charge of following up and making sure that everything works out all right, Eldridge. Looks like someone's thrown us a curveball," Doc lied.

Chapter 32

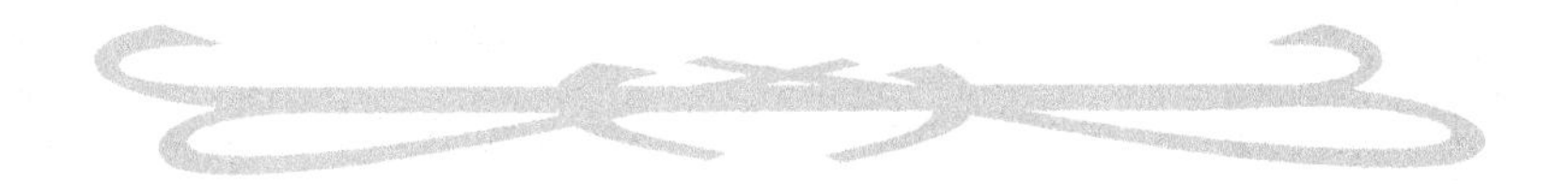

Eldridge looked at Doc and said, "Gimme one of those hand grenades."

"What for? I thought we'd decided not to use them right now."

"Well, look behind us. There's another car behind the one with those two damn spics in it."

Doc took out the scope again and looked through the back window. Sure enough, there was a third car. He couldn't tell who was in it because the car behind them was obstructing his vision.

"Dang, Eldridge, you're right, but I can't make out who it is. It could be just a tourist or someone going home."

The longer he stared at it, he couldn't help but notice it was having an unsettling effect on the two Hispanics, who slowed down to let the car pass. Doc placed the scope down and chastised Eldridge for calling the two Hispanics "spics." "Eldridge, I wish you wouldn't call those Hispanics 'spics' or names like that. How would you feel if they called you a 'smoke' or a 'gig' or maybe even the N word?"

Eldridge, who was now becoming more fractious, either out of fear or anger, said, "They probably call me worse than that when I'm not around, but if it'll make you feel better I'll just call them Mexicans."

"How do you know they're Mexicans? Do you know them very well?"

"Nope. Like I said, I had never seen them before I met 'em in the hotel lobby. All I know is that they work for the same firm; at least that's what Muhammed said. You know, he's the one that got all of us together like you wanted. Of course, before I went with him I checked with the man who hired me to work for you."

When the car that had been following the Hispanics pulled around them, Doc noticed through the scope that it was the woman from Lyon. He said with his voice quivering, "Dang, Eldridge, that's your girlfriend, the one that tried to kill you. I wonder how she caught up with us out here in the middle of nowhere."

Eldridge tried to peep through the rearview mirror to see if he could make out who was in the car. When he couldn't, he asked, his voice breaking up, "Are you sure?"

"Not absolutely, but almost. I guess she could be on the money trail too. Of course, that doesn't explain why she tried to do away with you, does it?"

"No, Mr. Gibbs, but I'll tell you one thing. When I get my hands on her, if you'll let me, she's gonna talk or else!"

"That's a good idea, son, but let's wait. Now hand me the hand grenade I gave you, in case she tries to pull up beside us. Shoot first and ask questions later. Of course, I don't think she will if she's after the money. I wonder who hired her. Surely she's not interested in either one of those two women, unless she has something in common with the Moises group from Peru or is a friend of the one who tried to do away with the no-good attorney. In any event, why don't we slow down and see what she does?"

Eldridge didn't particularly want to slow down. He bellowed out, "Hell, why don't we turn off at the next farmhouse, if there is one on this road, and see what happens? Surely she doesn't have as much heat as we've got."

"Probably not, probably not, but I don't think that's going to solve anything, because if she is following us she'll no doubt wait until we get back on the road again."

"Maybe not," Eldridge replied. "Those two Hispanics we met in Chicago might decide to take her out."

"Let's hope not, Eldridge, because if they do we'll never really know what she's up to or who she's working for."

"Damn, Mr. Gibbs, you mean to say you're gonna leave us out here on the road and let those people try to decide what they want to do to us, or are we gonna do something to take the initiative?"

"That's a good thought, Eldridge. I'll bet they're following us because they think we know exactly where Muhammed is. If that's the case, I doubt they'll do anything until we get there. One thing for sure, we know your girlfriend from Lyon is not on our side, but maybe the Hispanics are. So why don't you pull out that hog leg, and I'll get this little nine-millimeter Glock that I've got in the back and put it in my waistband and assemble my rifle. We'll just stop and see what happens."

When they reached a clearing at the top of the next hill, they pulled over to the side of the road and stopped. The woman in the car that had passed the two Hispanics had little recourse other than to pass them. When she did, Doc stuck his hand out the window and waved at her. Without a question, it was the so-called nun from Lyon.

When he waved, she turned her head to the right in an effort to keep him from recognizing her and drove as fast as she could over the hill.

The two Hispanics, who were stopped behind them, didn't move until Doc got out and motioned for them to approach. They drove up behind them, stopped, and got out. Sure enough, it was Sancho and his friend Ramon.

Doc, who was now so scared that he could barely speak, even with his voice amplified, managed to say, "What took you so long, men? I kinda had the idea that we would have gotten together way before we reached here. What are y'all up to? Are you after a cut of the money or after Muhammed or exactly what?"

Sancho gave him a sarcastic smile and answered, "We after money, don't you remember? There's two halves to the money; one half goes to the firm, and the other half is gonna end up in Muhammed's hands. Surely you do not think he'll give any to that Communist bitch, do you?"

"How in the hell do I know?" Eldridge said. "I don't know any of y'all. I just know Mr. Gibbs and the firm hired us to find the person who hired the Communist who tried to kill the attorney."

Before Eldridge could say anything else, Doc interrupted. "That's right. We're just following up to make sure Muhammed does as he was supposed to. As to the other half of the money, we're not sure what he's going to do with it or who has it. It could be that he hasn't made the transfer yet and it's still in the bank."

"I'll tell you what," Doc said. "Since you say you're here, on your own, why don't you pull that Peugeot off the road and get in the car with us, and we'll find Muhammed and see what he's done."

Sancho and Ramon didn't want to, but when they saw Eldridge's .44 Magnum, the sniper rifle, and the nine-millimeter Glock Doc had stuffed in his waistband, they decided that they had little choice.

"Good," Doc said with his voice quivering and his heart about to pound out of his chest. "Now get all your paraphernalia out of that Peugeot, and let's all go together since we're on the same team. We'll follow this map to where Muhammed supposedly is with the two women. He'll no doubt know where the other half of the money is."

They cleaned their belongings out of the Peugeot and placed them in the trunk of the Citroen.

Doc, playing a hunch, asked, "Where's your C-4 plastic? We don't want to leave it here."

They looked at each other and Sancho smiled. He said, "Oh, yes, Mr. Gibbs, thank you for reminding me. I was about to forget."

Eldridge spoke up in his deep baritone voice. "I bet you were."

This didn't seem to faze Sancho in the least. He smiled and went to get a large bag with the C-4 in it and placed it in the backseat.

Doc handed the map to Ramon and instructed them to sit up front and drive.

Eldridge turned to Doc and asked, "What about the woman?"

"Oh yeah," Doc said. "Do you men know the woman who passed you back there?"

They looked perplexed, and Sancho answered, "No, sir, Mr. Gibbs. No know woman. She's probably just some French woman on holiday."

"No, she's not a French woman on holiday. She's working with someone. We do not know who, and we need to be leery of her," Doc told them firmly.

Sancho's friend Ramon said, "As soon as we see her, do you want me to take her out, Mr. Gibbs?"

"No, I just want us to find out who she's with and what she's up to. She'll no doubt join us as soon as we pass where she's parked. That is, if she doesn't already know where Muhammed is. Do you men know that there are two other men in on this?"

They looked perplexed, and Sancho nervously asked, "No, what other men?"

"The two that went in the bank with the women to get the money. I don't know who they are, but I know wherever the women are, they are. So, we've got to be cautious. Do you guys know Muhammed?"

"No, sir, never met before we saw him in the hotel in Chicago. He just works for the same outfit."

Eldridge said, "Damn, that means that none of us know each other."

"That's right," Doc replied. "Though we will soon enough. Now just keep driving, Sancho, and let's go and get this over with. I'm sure the woman from Lyon that passed us has already called ahead to someone. How did she act when she passed y'all?"

"Oh, she never looked at us."

"Good. Maybe she'll tell whoever she called that there's just the two of us on the way—me and brother Eldridge. Are you guys very good with these plastic explosives?"

Sancho smiled and said, "Good enough, Mr. Gibbs. We used this type of firecracker a lot in Nicaragua a while back."

When he said that, Doc's heart stopped momentarily.

Chapter 33

THEY DROVE ON IN SILENCE for the next several miles before Eldridge spoke. "Mr. Gibbs, I thought you said that bitch from Lyon would join up with us. Where is she? If she's gonna follow us to where Muhammed is, she's either lost or has gone on ahead."

Doc took a deep breath and belched up part of the croissant he had eaten in Biarritz into the back of his throat and said, "Eldridge, she's gone on ahead. I'll bet she's made contact with someone who either knows where Muhammed is or is with him. What do you think, Sancho? Do you and Ramon have any ideas?"

"No, but don't worry. We will find her." He laughed.

Eldridge asked, "What's so funny?"

"Oh, nothing. We've dealt with people like her before. Right, Ramon?"

"Yeah. I only hope that the group she's with hasn't messed up our plan."

"What plan?" Eldridge asked in his deep baritone voice.

"Oh, the one that Mr. Gibbs has worked out. I'm sure he's got a very detailed plan."

"No, Sancho, I don't have a very detailed plan. But I'll tell you what, that woman is very dangerous. If you don't believe me, ask Eldridge."

"Oh, Mr. Gibbs," Eldridge moaned. "Why'd you bring that up?"

"I just think our two friends in the front seat need to know that she is a potential killer, that's all."

"How do you know she's a killer?" Sancho asked. "Do you reckon she could have been the one that had someone shoot up our car when we were following you to Biarritz?"

Doc cleared his throat and said, with his voice breaking up, "No, that was me. I didn't know who you were, but I knew you had been following us for quite some time, and all I wanted to do was disable the car. I'm sorry about that. Why didn't you let us know? That way we wouldn't have lost any time."

Ramon turned and looked at Eldridge and Doc in the backseat. He said, "You see that bag of explosives? If we hadn't gotten that out of the car when we jumped out and ran down the hill when it caught on fire, we wouldn't be here now."

"I'm sorry about that, men. I really and truly am. Somehow, someway, I'll make it up to you. Why did you think you had to follow us the way you did? Didn't you trust us?"

Sancho replied, "We don't trust anybody."

"That's a terrible thing," Doc said, "but I guess it's the rules of the game."

"Whatta you mean?" Eldridge asked.

"Ask Sancho. He'll tell you the same thing I've been telling you—that you can only trust yourself most of the time. However, there are times when you can't trust yourself. That's when you need to validate what you're thinking with someone else. That seems to be the situation we're in now. We've got to depend on each other until we accomplish our mission. Right, Sancho?"

"Yeah."

"Okay. We'll do that until the mission is complete. After that, I just hope we can walk away from each other with the satisfaction of knowing we have done what we set out to do, plus have the other half of the money and split it up. I can assure you of one thing: I'm not going to hurt any of y'all, and I hope y'all feel the same way about me."

The Hispanics looked at Eldridge and said, "You in on this all the way, Eldridge? Just the four of us and maybe Muhammed and some of his friends?"

"Yeah, I guess so. What other choice do we have?"

"Oh," Doc replied. "We can always stop right now and turn around and go back."

"That's no option, Mr. Gibbs. I'm gonna get that woman from Lyon," Eldridge bellowed.

Sancho smiled and laughed before saying, "Exactly what did she do to you, Eldridge—if that's your name—to make you hate her so much? It's not good to hate. Just think of her as someone that is expendable."

Ramon commented, "That's right. We're all expendable, but in this case the ones that are on the other side are all more expendable. We'll just take care of them and be on our way."

"What makes you so sure that we'll be able to take care of them?" Doc asked.

"Oh, my buddy Sancho and I have been in worse situations. That bag between you and your big black friend, along with the weapons we have, if used properly, can take care of most anything we run into, if we don't make the mistake of ending up in the middle of the wrong crowd before we realize it."

"Good, Ramon. I don't think we'll end up in the middle of the wrong crowd. Where are we on the map now?" Sancho asked unemotionally.

Doc handed the map back over the seat to Sancho, pointed his finger to a spot on the map, and answered, "Right here."

"That means that we are only about four miles away. You know I'm too old to walk very far with my bad ankle, so we're gonna have to get a lot closer. I only hope that they don't have a lookout posted somewhere before we get to within a few hundred yards of where they are."

"Don't worry," Ramon said as he pulled out his long switchblade. "Before we get there, I'll go ahead and check and, if necessary, eliminate them."

"Eliminate them?" Eldridge blurted out.

"Oh, yeah, cut throat," he said as he made a motion as if he was cutting his throat.

"Yeah," Sancho commented. "Maybe the one you cut throat, will have some communication equipment and weapons we can use."

Doc now knew for certain that he and Eldridge were in the wrong place at the wrong time. They were with two professionals who would just as soon kill someone as they would shake their hand. He got the map back and instructed them on what to do next.

"Take the next road to the left. If this map is correct it will put us within several hundred yards of them."

Ramon reached in his coat pocket and pulled out a .22-caliber pistol that was frequently used by assassins at short range, screwed the silencer on it, and told Sancho to let him out before they got to the left turn. He didn't want to use the pistol but would if he couldn't use his knife.

Doc couldn't help but ask why.

"Oh, Mr. Gibbs, that's probably where they'll have their first lookout, if indeed they have one."

"What if it's one of Muhammed's people?" Eldridge asked.

Sancho was quick to add that it didn't make any difference who it was. They would just get rid of them.

This made Doc belch, and he could taste the croissant in the back of his mouth again. When he recovered enough to speak, he asked how they would know that he had taken care of anyone who might be stationed as a lookout.

He took out his cell phone and said that he would call Sancho when it was time for them to move up and that he would join them at the turn in the road.

Eldridge thought about what Doc had said earlier, about him being in the wrong game, and realized that it was a fact. These two Hispanics were real pros, and he was just an ordinary guy who carried out routine missions. In fact, he had never really shot anyone in his life.

Chapter 34

WHEN THEY REACHED THE PLACE where Ramon wanted to get out, he told Sancho to stop and that he would see them shortly. Then he left through the woods.

Doc, not wanting to show his ignorance or appear to be the leader, didn't say much, except to ask Sancho what he'd paid for the Renault.

Sancho was quick to inform him that he hadn't paid anything for it; they had stolen it.

"Oh, okay," Doc said. "That means I won't have to pay you for the car, only for the discomfort and inconvenience I've caused you. Then again, I probably should pay you for the Peugeot."

"Oh, no, Mr. Gibbs, we stole it and changed license plates. We will not have to worry about it until we get back, if we plan to come back this way."

"Okay, I'll tell you what. Brother Eldridge and I will make it up to you. We'll make sure you're richly rewarded for your inconvenience. You don't reckon the police or anyone knows which direction you took after you stole it, do you?"

"No, I don't think so. They probably haven't even missed it yet. They were too busy making out on the beach to notice."

"Oh, you got it from a young couple."

"Yeah, a couple of French boys from Paris. At least, that's what their papers say."

"Hmm," Doc said. "These French sure do have their ways about doing things, don't they, Eldridge?"

Eldridge looked dumbfounded. "Whatta you mean? I don't know anything about French boys. The only people I've met here are the women from Barcelona that we got to go with us to the bank and that French woman in Lyon who tried to kill me."

Sancho laughed again. "How did she try to kill you, Eldridge, or whatever your name is?"

"That's my business. You just keep your eye on the road and listen for Ramon to phone," Eldridge snarled.

Doc intervened before things got out of hand by telling Sancho, "Eldridge caught her trying to put something in his cognac in order to try and conceal her identity." This satisfied Sancho and tended to calm Eldridge.

After waiting for about thirty minutes, Sancho's phone rang. It was Ramon telling him that it was all clear for them to move ahead and that he would join them shortly.

Sancho turned off his phone, placed it in his coat pocket, and said, "Mr. Gibbs, with your permission we'll proceed on. I've gotten the all clear."

Eldridge, who had never really liked the two spics, as he called them, got out the .44 Magnum and pointed it at Sancho's back through the seat.

Doc wasn't sure what Eldridge might do. All he knew was that Eldridge seemed to be about as scared as he was.

In order to change the subject and try to calm Eldridge, he asked him if he noticed anything peculiar about the girl from Lyon.

"No, not particularly. Why do you ask?"

"For starters, she was pigeon-toed and she didn't shave her legs as well as some of the girls stateside. Did she shave her armpits?"

Eldridge grabbed his lower lip, pulled on it, and thoughtfully replied, "Come to think of it, Mr. Gibbs, I'm not real sure. Why do you ask?"

"Oh, I was just trying to get a better fix on her. You know, some of the women in different parts of the country don't always shave under their arms."

"Oh, I didn't know that," Eldridge said.

Sancho spoke up. "Maybe she is one of those Marxist, Leninist bitches. You know, the nudist, vegetarian group that goes around reading about Marx and some of their other gods. Many of the ones we ran into in South America didn't shave anything except occasionally their heads."

This shocked Eldridge. How had he overlooked the fact that she may have shaved underneath her arms? Why hadn't he noticed that she was pigeon-toed like Doc had said? He asked, "What else did you notice about her, Mr. Gibbs?"

"Not much, other than she was wearing Birkenstock sandals. That might not mean anything, since they are German sandals and a world of people wear 'em, particularly the hippy group from the sixties and seventies."

"Oh," Eldridge said.

Sancho started to laugh and told them that many of the ones that he knew from Central and South America wore combat boots. They didn't wear Birkenstocks or any other kind of sandals. It had been his experience, he said, that Birkenstocks were limited mostly to the people in Europe and the United States.

Doc knew they did sell a lot more in Europe and the United States, along with the standard earth shoes, and said, "Well, forget it, men. Make a left turn here, if you don't mind, Sancho."

"Okay, boss," Sancho said as he turned off to the left only to be met in the middle of the road by his partner, Ramon.

When Ramon got in the car, Sancho looked over at him, smiled, and asked, "How did it go?"

"Fine."

Eldridge could hardly contain himself and had to ask, "Whatta you mean, fine? Did you run into anyone?"

"Oh, just one dead Arab."

Doc asked what he did to him, and Ramon said, "Nothing. Someone had already killed him."

When he said that, both Doc and Eldridge became nauseated but didn't say anything.

Sancho laughed. "Which side do you think that dud was on?"

"What difference does it make? Not on any side now," Ramon answered. "Eldridge's woman probably shot him."

Doc wanted Sancho to pull the car over to the side of the road and let him vomit, but he knew better than to ask. He and Eldridge just remained quiet until they got to the point where they thought they should get out and try to walk to where they needed to go.

Before they had traveled a hundred yards through the woods, they noticed a Peugeot hidden in the bushes. Doc assumed that this was the one that the girl from Lyon had been driving and mentioned it to the others.

Sancho whispered, "What should we do now, Mr. Gibbs?"

Doc didn't want to sound uncertain and told them that he thought they should look for her before going any farther.

"If she's really with Muhammed and the rest of them, she would have driven on up to where they are staying. I'm pretty sure that she's waiting for someone to join her."

Sancho smiled, laughed, and said softly, "Well, we're here. I think I'll go find her. She can't be far."

With that, he pulled out a roll of duct tape that he had tucked in his oversized coat and sneaked off up through the brush next to the path.

A short time later, he returned and told them that he thought he had Eldridge's mystery lady bound and ready to go. With that, they proceeded on up the path toward the small two-story stone cottage where there were eight or ten Arab men and two women dressed in Arab garb.

The Arabs were talking to Muhammed and the two men who had taken the women to the bank and transferred the money. Doc and his group loaded their weapons and walked on up to them.

Ramon, who was a lot larger than Sancho, had placed the woman Sancho had found along the side of the road, staring at the cottage through a pair of binoculars, over his back. They approached Muhammed and the group, as if they were expected guests.

Muhammed seemed somewhat surprised but tried to act as if he was glad to see them. The two French-looking men didn't know quite what to say, and the Arabs seemed to be frightened.

This sent a chill over Doc and Eldridge, but not Sancho or Ramon. It seemed that they weren't scared of the devil himself.

They introduced themselves, and Ramon told them he had another concubine for them. The Arab who seemed to be in charge pulled the duct tape off of her mouth and examined her teeth. They weren't sure why he was examining her teeth until Muhammed told them that they were checking to see if she was in good shape.

The sight of the so-called girl from Lyon made Eldridge mad enough to want to choke her, but Doc held him back and said, "Later, son, later. Let's see what's going on."

Muhammed asked the Arab leader what he would give him for this particular woman. He told him that as far as he was concerned, she was of little value and told Muhammed he would be glad to ship her out if he wanted to get rid of her.

Doc told Muhammed that all he knew was that she was dangerous and worked for some other group. When they found her she had them staked out and was probably waiting on some of her friends to arrive.

When he said that, the Arab leader told Muhammed he wanted no part of the wild woman.

Muhammed restrained her until the next time someone arrived with the opium and cigarettes.

Ramon placed another piece of duct tape over her mouth and dumped her on the ground next to the stone cottage. He said, "I guess we get rid of her."

Doc interrupted and said, "Let's wait and see if she's really called some of her friends, and then we can let Eldridge decide what to do."

Sancho and Ramon told Doc that it had been quite some time since they had been with a woman and asked if they could have their way with her before they shipped out.

This was unconscionable to Doc, and he said, "Let's wait and see what happens. Did you get her cell phone, Ramon? We might be having guests anytime now."

"Yes, sir, Mr. Gibbs," he said as he handed him a rather sophisticated cell phone, which was on a different frequency from the ones they had.

Doc had Muhammed ask the Arabs where they thought intruders were more likely to come from in the event that some of her friends showed up.

They pointed out the vulnerable locations in the area. Sancho asked Eldridge for the explosives he had brought up to the cottage, and he and Ramon started placing them in the locations the Arabs had pointed out. The Arabs told Muhammed that occasionally a helicopter delivered cigarettes and opium to them, so they should be extremely careful in the placement of explosives around the helicopter's landing site.

After they had finished placing the explosives, Muhammed had the Arabs tie up the two women in Arab dress and put them in the cottage.

Doc and Eldridge found a spot where, if anyone landed by helicopter, they would be able to shoot it down if necessary, or at least when it tried to take off.

Sancho, Ramon, and the rest of them remained around the open fire, as if nothing was going on.

It was a good thing, because several minutes later a helicopter did arrive.

Muhammed asked if that was the one that usually brought the opium and cigarettes. The Arab in charge assured him that it wasn't.

They drew their weapons, sat, and waited. When it landed, two armed men got off with grenades strapped around their waists and automatic rifles, ducked behind the stone wall, and pointed the rifles in the direction of the crowd sitting around the fire.

Sancho pulled the pin on the hand grenade that he had gotten earlier from Doc and heaved it in their direction. Muhammed and the others ran inside the cottage. It had a profound effect, in that it exploded the two men behind the fence and caused the pilot to start the helicopter and make an attempt to take off. When he did, Doc aimed the sniper rifle and placed a shot in the region of the tail rotor, thus disabling it. He reloaded and put a second shot in the same area.

When he did, the helicopter started whirling around out of control and ended up crashing down the hill.

Muhammed and his Arab friends came out of the cottage, went to check on the two armed men who had gotten off the helicopter, and found what was left of them. It wasn't much, since the grenades they had strapped on them had exploded.

Sancho and Ramon went down the hillside to recover the pilot from the helicopter. When they arrived, he was still alive. Working frantically they were able to rescue him, along with several rockets and launchers, before fire engulfed the helicopter.

They dragged the semiconscious pilot up the hill. After he had recovered enough to answer questions, Sancho, in an alarming tone of voice, shouted, "It's truth time."

"Ramon, go get Eldridge's girlfriend so we can have a chat with both of them at the same time. Sancho's right. It is truth time," Doc said, trying to sound more confident than he really was.

Chapter 35

RAMON BROUGHT THE GIRL FROM Lyon over next to the fire, dropped her on the stone patio like she was a bag of oats, and removed the duct tape from her mouth.

Angrily, Eldridge shouted, "Who in the hell are you, and who do you work for? Why'd you try to kill me?"

She snarled and spat on him, causing him to draw his arm back to slap her. Doc grabbed his arm as it started to move forward and was lifted off his feet and flung onto the stone patio, causing his sunglasses and fez to fall off.

Everyone was shocked by the sight of the huge black man hurling the man they thought was in charge of the operation through the air like he was a rag doll.

Startled, Eldridge dropped to his knees and, with his deep baritone voice breaking up, said, "I'm sorry, Mr. Gibbs. You know I would never do anything to hurt you."

Before Eldridge could help him up, the girl from Lyon tried to kick him and shouted, "Why did you leave that sex toy in that Volkswagen for me, you black bastard? That old man should have you killed."

Ramon pulled out his switchblade, placed it at Eldridge's throat, and asked Doc what he wanted him to do.

"Nothing. I'm okay," he moaned. "We need to have a frank discussion with this young lady and the pilot before more of their friends arrive."

"Okay, Mr. Gibbs," Muhammed replied with a sadistic smile on his face. "Why don't we turn them over to my Arab brothers? They know how to make them talk."

"If you promise they won't kill them in the process."

"Sure thing, Mr. Gibbs. Why don't you and Eldridge go inside and talk to the two women we brought here?"

Doc wasn't sure what he was up to, but he felt Muhammed didn't want them around during the interrogation for some reason. Anyway, he needed to check on the two women in Arab dress who were in the cottage, and he reluctantly did as Muhammed suggested.

The minute Eldridge and Doc entered the cottage, the Arabs removed the pilot's clothing, bound his ankles together and his arms behind him, and placed him face down on the ground. They then started beating the soles of his feet with a shepherd's crook until the pain became so excruciating he lost control of his bladder and passed out. Next, they tied him to a post, doused him with water, and left him in the cold breeze until he recovered enough to talk.

While this was going on, the two French-looking men removed the girl's clothing, blindfolded her, strapped her to a board with her kicking and screaming, lowered her slowly into the watering trough, and held her underwater until she had to breathe. The moment she started to inhale a little water, they removed her, and when she stopped coughing, they asked her how she liked her swim.

She coughed and shouted that she wasn't going to tell them anything until they told her what had happened to Marta Roho.

The older of the two men said, "First you must answer a few questions for us. You do understand this, don't you, my dear?"

Before she could answer, they submerged her in the water until she could no longer hold her breath again. After the fourth time, she was ready to talk. "I'm a member of the Red Brigade, and some of my friends are on the way. They'll be arriving shortly to take care of you."

"Good. We shall be waiting for them, dear," the older of the two men said.

"Do you want to go for another swim while we're waiting?"

"No, no!" she screamed. She was cold and wet and afraid of what would happen if they decided to leave her underwater.

"If you'll give me Marta Roho, I'll get them to call off the operation."

"Thanks, but no thanks," the younger of the two men said. "I think we'll wait and see what your friends have in mind." They slowly submerged her in the water again.

Doc had heard the beating and the woman screaming from the cottage and told Eldridge, "You remember what I told you earlier. We're in the wrong game with the wrong people. We're in a league with the devil, and as soon as we get out of this mess, I'm going to retire, and I certainly hope you'll give it consideration."

"Oh, Mr. Gibbs," Eldridge said with his deep baritone voice, "they're not going to hurt them very bad. At least that's what Muhammed said."

"I know what he said, but I've never believed him. That's why I'm here. The deal was for him to transfer half the money to the outfit and leave half of it for the Maoist, Marta Roho, to travel around France and spew her Communist hatred. But before I go and check on Muhammed and the others, let's see who these two women in Arab dress are and what's been happening to them."

Eldridge untied them and removed their burkas. Their heads were shaved, and they were blindfolded, gagged, and had their social security numbers tattooed on their pale, gaunt faces. They didn't make a move. They just sat there, staring blindly into space. It was an appalling sight that made Doc's heart race and Eldridge to become mute. Neither had seen two seemingly blind women with their heads shaved and their social security numbers tattooed on their forehead before with the soles of their feet and hands swollen and bleeding.

Doc told Eldridge to watch them while he went to the well and got a dipper of water for them to drink. They refused the water and pointed outside.

Eldridge looked at Doc and said, "What in the hell's going on here?"

"I'm not sure. Maybe they want us to ask the Arabs or someone if it's all right for them to drink."

"What do you mean, Mr. Gibbs?"

"I mean what I said. They are probably not allowed to do anything without checking with their new husbands and getting their permission. It seems that Muhammed has done what he was talking about in the hotel room, rather than what he was supposed to do. I hope not many members in the outfit are like Muhammed. My goodness, son, they have not followed the rules that we set forth, and someone must pay. Now watch them while I go get Muhammed."

When Doc stepped outside, he saw Muhammed, Sancho, and Ramon smoking a clove cigarette and watching the Arabs interrogate the pilot, and he saw the two French-looking men having the time of their life, submerging the girl from Lyon in the watering trough in between questions.

Doc's first reaction was to shout for them to stop, but instead he fired his rifle into the air and told them that if they didn't stop what they were doing, he was going to have them killed.

This was not true, but the old man had reached his limit. He was frightened, but at the same time he was very angry at their inhumanity.

The startled French-looking men and Arabs stopped what they were doing, came over, and joined them around the fire. He told Sancho and Ramon to shoot them if they moved.

Muhammed was surprised to see his reaction, as were the others. Sancho and Ramon, who were not affected by Doc's outburst and did exactly what he said, took the automatic rifles that had been retrieved from the helicopter and held them at bay while Doc asked them exactly what they thought they were doing.

The younger of the two French-looking men told him in broken English that they were only carrying out his orders.

"What orders? I only told you to have a talk with them, not kill them. We can excuse our Arab brothers for not knowing any different, but certainly you do," Doc angrily said.

Doc then turned to Muhammed and let him know how disappointed he was in him for going to such extremes.

"What do you mean, Mr. Gibbs?" Muhammed asked.

"Go inside and look at the two women, and you'll see exactly what I mean. From what I've seen thus far, I predict that you want to have a very long life span. You were only supposed to transfer half the money and leave the other for Marta Roho. I believe you have sold them to the Arabs. Since they are so frightened they won't even talk. Now exactly, what did you do?"

"I gave them both to the Arabs for brides rather than disposing of them."

"You were never supposed to dispose of them. You were supposed to follow orders, as stated. One woman was to be left to work the remainder of her days doing manual labor, and the other one was to be allowed to roam free as long as she did not leave France."

"Exactly what sort of training are they in?"

"They're breaking them in to be good brides and to herd goats."

"Well, where are the goats? I haven't seen a goat since I've been here. Have you, Sancho, or you, Ramon?"

"No, Mr. Gibbs," Sancho said.

Muhammed answered, "They're in the meadow below the other side of the cottage, and the women have been doing a very good job in the brief time they've been here."

"Why are they blindfolded and gagged?" Doc asked.

"Since they are non-Arab women," Muhammed said, "they have to go through a period of training. Like I said, they have been good at herding the goats and waiting on the men and keeping their mouths shut."

"You're right. They've been keeping their mouths shut. They've been gagged," Doc retorted.

Suddenly one of the Arabs started yelling in Arabic to the others.

Ramon pointed his rifle at him and said, "Gimme the word, Mr. Gibbs."

"No, son, hold it. Muhammed, what's got them so scared?"

Muhammed jumped up, turned toward Dr. Suggs, and said, "They say we've got guests."

"Guests?" Whatta you mean?"

"The people the woman from Lyon told us about are coming to rescue Marta Roho, I guess," Muhammed said as he threw down his cigarette.

Doc forgot about the two women inside and called out to Eldridge to come and take his position. The Arabs spread out around the perimeter with their World War II German Mausers, and Sancho armed the explosives while Ramon and Eldridge went up to the second floor of the cottage, where they could get a better view of the meadow below.

Muhammed stayed with Doc and asked him what he wanted him to do.

"For starters, bind the pilot and the so-called woman from Lyon together with the man's right leg tied to the woman's left leg, and do the same with their arms. Turn them loose in the direction we came from."

Muhammed, breathing deeply and rapidly, asked, "Why?"

"Because I want them to lead us to where their friends are. When they see them they will no doubt show themselves. Our Arab friends and Eldridge and Ramon will have things covered from the other direction—that is, unless the intruders have rocket launchers."

"Rocket launchers?" Muhammed shouted.

"Yes. These people are every bit as bad as some of the people we are working with. They kill just to be killing."

This shocked Muhammed, who gave him a startled look and emphatically replied, "I've never killed anyone. It is true, I have tortured some people in order to get them to talk, but I've never killed anyone."

"That's good to know, Muhammed," Doc snarled. "Now here we are with a bunch of people who would just as soon kill you as say hello, and none of us have ever killed anyone, unless Ramon and Sancho have. Seems like we are in one more heck of a mess. Now go tie them together and turn them loose."

Muhammed bound the man and woman from Lyon, as Doc suggested, and let them run as best they could, bound together, in the direction Doc thought their friends would be coming from. It wasn't long before they heard several shots and screams.

Chapter 36

The battle was now under way. The first shots came from the direction in which the woman and the pilot had run. On the other side of the cottage the disturbed goats were beginning to come back up the hill. This meant they were surrounded. Doc's only hope was that the Arabs had given Sancho accurate information as to where to place the explosives. The last thing he wanted was to get involved in any sort of battle, but if it came to that it would have to be what Eldridge had said earlier: "If it comes down to either us or them, I'd rather it be them than us."

All of a sudden the two French-looking men, who had been momentarily lost, started speaking to each other in German.

Doc shouted, "Muhammed, exactly who are these two that you hired to get the money out of the bank?"

"Oh, they're runaway French legionnaires from Germany."

Doc knew that the French legionnaires were not supposed to be in France and asked no further questions. It was now time to defend themselves.

Doc zeroed in his rifle, and the minute he saw one of the members of the Red Brigade, he shot, hitting him midchest.

The others with him didn't seem to be fazed and proceeded up the hill.

Doc reloaded his rifle and watched them through the scope, wondering when Sancho planned to set off the explosives. He didn't have to wait long. Sancho dialed in the first two and exploded them, creating havoc.

On the other side of the cottage, coming up from the meadow, were at least three people. Ramon left Eldridge, rushed downstairs to Sancho, and told him. Sancho instructed Ramon to go back upstairs and dial him on his cell phone as soon as they got within a couple hundred yards.

In the meantime, Marta Roho slipped out of the house and started to make a break for it. When she did, one of the Arabs grabbed her and started to beat her.

Doc shouted for him to let her go. The Arab did as he was instructed by Muhammed, and she rushed down the hill toward the meadow.

Ramon dialed Sancho and calmly told him that there were at least three men, plus one of the women who had been held captive by the Arabs, within a couple hundred yards of the house.

Sancho set off three more explosives. This resulted in bodies and body parts flying through the air. One of the French legionnaires aimed a rocket at a car he saw down the hill and fired it. It demolished the car and caused pieces of flying metal to hit two more of the intruders.

Doc spotted one that was getting dangerously close to the house and shot him between the eyes. This caused Doc to become extremely nauseated and throw up.

In the meantime, Muhammed had done nothing other than light another clove-scented cigarette and start to smoke.

When Doc recovered from shooting the intruder, he directed Muhammed to come inside and watch the other woman who had apparently not moved since they had left her unguarded in the house.

Eldridge, who was not a very good shot, took out the .44 Magnum and started firing in the direction of the three remaining intruders coming up from the meadow with the goats. He accidentally hit two of them. The other one was taken out by the Arabs.

Following this, there was a break in the action, and silence ensued. Doc couldn't help but wonder whether they had gotten all of them or if some of them had retreated.

After a prolonged silence, the two French legionnaires asked Muhammed if he wanted them to check to see if any intruders were still there.

Doc instructed Muhammed to tell them to go ahead if they felt like they were up to it. Doc knew he wasn't and was pretty sure Eldridge wasn't either. Ramon might, or Sancho might, but he needed them here—Ramon as a spotter and Sancho to set off the explosives.

Doc told them that they might be running the risk of being hit by friendly fire and suggested that they take off their shirts so that they could be differentiated from the intruders.

They followed orders without hesitation and slowly made their way down the hillside the way Doc, Eldridge, Ramon, and Sancho had originally approached the cottage. A short time later they returned with a body count of six, as best they could tell, since some of them had been blown to pieces by the explosives.

Muhammed asked the Germans what had happened to the girl and the pilot.

"Oh, they got shot by their own people. They were the first ones shot. Didn't you hear them scream?"

Doc, overcome with fear, asked, "What about the side of the cottage down by the meadow and the other side of the helicopter pad?"

Muhammed volunteered to check the side where the helicopter pad was, and the two legionnaires worked their way down toward the meadow. They found only parts of four bodies. From talking to Eldridge and Ramon, there were two, maybe three, still missing.

Muhammed instructed the Arabs, who knew the terrain like the palm of their hand, to accompany him down the hill by the helicopter pad and around to the right toward the meadow.

Doc and the others waited. A short time later they retuned and told them that there were five, rather than the three mentioned by Eldridge and Ramon, and they had taken care of them. Doc was afraid to ask what they had done to them, but he thought he knew. They had used their knives to cut their throats.

Sancho, who was having the time of his life setting off the explosives, asked, "What's next, Mr. Gibbs? Do you think there are any more left?"

"I don't know, Sancho, but let's wait and see. I think I'll see if I can make my way up to the second floor and look around. Here, take these three grenades in case any of the group are left."

Doc slowly made it up the steps to the second floor with his bad ankle bleeding from rubbing on the metal brace. He made a 360-degree sweep of the terrain with his scope. He spotted one person dressed like the other intruders starting to get in their Citroen and leave. He called out to the French legionnaires, hoping that they would see if they couldn't capture whoever it was before he managed to hot-wire the car and leave. Rather than doing that, they took out a rocket launcher and blew up the Citroen with him in it.

This caused Doc's heart to leap into his throat, and it caused him to become weak and fall back against the wall opposite the window. How was he going to get out of there? He couldn't walk, and there were no other vehicles left.

After making sure they were completely safe, the Arabs roasted the goats that had been killed during the gunfight for their evening meal. The goat tasted like goat, which wasn't too bad if you were hungry, but Doc was too nauseated and frightened to eat, even if he'd had Worcestershire sauce, so he sat alone and thought about what they had done.

Chapter 37

Eldridge came over to where Doc was sitting and asked, "Mr. Gibbs, what's the matter? Aren't you gonna eat?"

Doc looked at him and, making good eye contact, responded to his questions. "Eldridge, I never did like goat, even barbecued goat the way we used to eat on the Fourth of July when I was growing up. I'm just sitting here trying to figure out why in the world we got mixed up in this and exactly who all the people were we killed. I know one was the girl from Lyon, whoever she was, and another was Marta Roho, the so-called girl from Ipanema. As to the pilot and the men who came to rescue her, I have no idea who they were, nor do I have any idea as to whether or not the backup that was called in were really members of the Red Brigade."

"How so?" Eldridge asked.

"I'm not sure the Red Brigade even exists any longer, and if it does there aren't very many of them left. But, be that as it may, this group is no longer with us. I wonder who the other Caucasian woman is that's waiting hand and foot on the men while they eat. She must be Jenny with the light-brown hair, who hired Roho and her bunch of Maoists to knock off the attorney."

What Eldridge said next was shocking. "Mr. Gibbs, according to Muhammed and the two French legionnaires, her real name is Ginger Bigelow."

When he said this, Doc jumped up and shouted, "My goodness, are you sure of that, Eldridge? If it's the Ginger Bigelow I'm thinking about, at one time she was having a tempestuous affair with the attorney that Roho tried to kill. That makes me wonder. Why would she want to kill him, unless she was angry over having to leave the States when her elderly husband died?

Huh, life's funny, Eldridge. Mrs. Bigelow sure left for parts unknown not long after her husband died a rather untimely death, I should say. He had a stroke at home one evening after he came in from work. That was about the same time his daughter, Lady Dee, and her boyfriend, Dr. Rupert Lowell, died on a trip to the Amazon. I guess, but I don't know, if the woman is Ginger Bigelow, she could be involved someway in their deaths. Oh forget about it, Eldridge, we'll have a little talk with her if the Arabs will let us after they get through eating."

Chapter 38

Doc was amazed at how the so-called Jenny with the light-brown hair scurried about, waiting on the men during the evening meal. It appeared to him that she wasn't doing it out of fright, and he thought, *Maybe she's learned to accept this type of lifestyle in the short time she's been with them. Then again, it could be that she really likes the Arab Muhammed gave her to.*

He called Muhammed over as soon as he finished eating and asked him to have a seat.

Muhammed sat down next to Doc and Eldridge and asked, "Mr. Gibbs, what's bothering you? You're not hungry?"

"No, I'm not hungry for goat, but I'm kinda hungry to find out what's been going on and exactly what's what and who's who. Now tell me what you know about this group of humanity, particularly the woman dressed in Arab garb."

Muhammed gave Doc a steely look, which made Eldridge want to choke him. Doc placed his hand on Eldridge's forearm to restrain him and said in his amplified voice, "Muhammed, let's start with first things first. Who is this woman? Is her name really Ginger Bigelow? Was she the one who hired Roho? And what do you know about the woman from Lyon?"

"What difference does it make?" Muhammed tersely answered.

When he said that, Eldridge pulled out the .44 Magnum and placed it in his lap, pointing at Muhammed. Doc said, as softly as he could, "Muhammed, no one is going to tell what you and your friends from the foreign legion and whoever else is involved did with the other half of the money. I just need to know the straight story. I mainly need to know who this woman is. Would you mind calming down while you still have the chance, before my friend

Eldridge here gets all riled up, and asking the Arab you gave her to if I can have a word with her? It's critical because she could be the one who hired Marta Roho and the ex-Maoists to kill the attorney. After I have a little talk with her, we can get together with the others who were involved in stealing the money that was supposed to go to Roho. You know, the way it looks to me, Muhammed—and I want you to think about it for a long time before you consider doing what you may have in mind—if we split the money that didn't go to the outfit, we'll all be culpable, and therefore we'll all have to keep our mouths shut and look after each other."

"Look after each other?" Muhammed replied.

"Yes, surely you understand that by taking the other half of the money we're in deep trouble, because we were supposed to give it to Roho. But if we split it up and no one finds out about it and we all come out of this alive, I'm sure things will work out just fine. However, there's one catch to it. If someone harms any of us, the others will no doubt report whoever does it to the powers that be, and that'll be a rather nasty mess, won't it?"

"Yes, sir," Muhammed quickly replied.

Eldridge was intrigued by what was going on but remained mute with his .44 Magnum still pointed at Muhammed.

Doc called Sancho and Ramon to join them. They placed down the fermented goat's milk they had been drinking and joined Doc, Eldridge, and Muhammed.

Sancho immediately turned to Doc and asked, "Mr. Gibbs, what do we do next?"

"Split the money that you and Ramon have been chasing."

Eldridge spoke up for the first time in his deep baritone voice. "Mr. Gibbs, how can we be sure that these two were following us for the money?"

Doc made a wild guess. "I can't think of any other reason for them to be following us. Aren't we all over here for the money? Isn't that right, Sancho?"

"Yes, Mr. Gibbs," Sancho said and smiled.

Ramon vehemently replied, "Why else would we be here? Surely you don't think we thought Muhammed was going to give that woman from South America any money. Anyway, we like money as well as anyone else, and we want our share. Isn't that right, Sancho?"

Sancho smiled. "Yes, that's why we were following you. We weren't sure exactly where Muhammed would go, but when we located you and your big black buddy, we knew we were on the right trail. All we knew was that Muhammed was supposed to take Roho and the other woman to a bank in the south of France."

Eldridge growled, "Mr. Gibbs, how do those two damn Germans figure in this operation?"

"I don't know, Eldridge. Maybe we should ask Muhammed."

Muhammed was somewhat uncertain as to where he stood with them. He figured he might be able to depend on the two French legionnaires, but he wasn't sure. As far as the Arabs were concerned, all he knew was that he couldn't cross them and he couldn't afford to tell them about the money. His deal with them had been to give them the women for future favors. The uncertainty caused him to make a decision not to cross the man who he thought was Mr. Gibbs, since he didn't know how high he ranked in the outfit.

Doc, who was still nauseated, frightened, and severely distressed about what he had gotten into by messing with Swindle and Turner, said, "Call the two Legionnaires over and let's see how we're going to make them split the money and if you are not going to give any to the Arabs."

Muhammed quickly answered, "That's right. I only gave the Arab brothers both women rather than giving any money. You know we couldn't turn Roho loose with that much money. The Legionnaires aren't in it for the money. They are just repaying a debt they owe me."

"Okay, we'll have to live with that. Now call the Legionnaires over before we decide on the split," Doc said, not sure Muhammed was being truthful.

Sancho and Ramon still had their automatic rifles they had removed from the helicopter, as well as the plastic explosives and the grenades that Doc had given them earlier. They readied themselves in case they ran into resistance from Muhammed and the Legionnaires.

When the Legionnaires came over and took a seat next to them, they confirmed that they didn't take part in the operation for the woman's money.

Doc still wasn't sure they were leveling with him and asked, "Why are you not interested in the money?"

The younger of the two Legionnaires replied, "It is of little consequence to us. We owe Muhammed and the firm a favor. Are you the one in charge of this operation?"

Doc didn't know what to say but answered, "Yes, for the time being. Why do you ask?"

The older of the two replied, "No particular reason. Anyway, we're more interested in the drug business than a small amount of money. We were just doing this to stay on good terms with you and the rest of the firm. You know, in case there's something else we may need help with later on."

The younger of the two piped up, "Yeah, the left hand washes the right hand. You help us, we help you."

"Good. We'll make a four-way split," Doc hastily replied without thinking.

Muhammed said, "Four ways? There are five of us."

Doc quickly replied, "I already have my money."

"Oh, you got a part of the other half," Eldridge naively said, thinking that part of the half that went to the outfit was to go to Doc.

Doc countered, "Don't worry about it, Eldridge, everything will come out fine when we get back. If I don't get back, something else will happen."

Eldridge knew what he was talking about, but the others didn't and assumed that if they didn't go along with him they would no doubt vanish like several of their other so-called friends had in the past when they crossed the outfit.

Chapter 39

Doc asked Muhammed again to ask the Arab, to whom he had given Ginger Bigelow, to join him.

"Why do you need to talk to him?" Muhammed asked.

"I need to get his permission to talk to the woman and see whether or not she wants to return to the States and face trial or stay here."

"Why did you change your mind, Mr. Gibbs? I thought you wanted her to spend the rest of her life working and living in poverty."

"I do. I just want to check and make sure that we've made the right decision."

"Okay, I'll go get Abdul."

"Do it. Of course, you'll have to stay with me and be an interpreter, since I doubt he speaks English."

When Abdul came over, Doc asked everyone to leave except Muhammed. He then told Abdul that, with his permission, he would like to speak to his woman.

Abdul said something in Arabic, and Muhammed interpreted.

"He says, Mr. Gibbs, that you can talk to her, but he doesn't wish to get rid of her, since she's making an excellent wife."

"Good. Ask him if I can remove her headdress so that I can identify her and make sure that she's the right one."

Muhammed asked Abdul, who responded in Arabic.

"What did he say, Muhammed?" Doc asked.

"It's against their custom, but since you were so generous to give him the fine woman, he will let us take her inside and remove the burka so you can identify her and ask her a few questions. But he does not wish to give her up."

With that, they went into the cottage, and Abdul instructed her to remove her burka. There she was, pale, gaunt, her head shaved, and her social security numbers tattooed on her forehead. She looked tired and frightened. Doc wasn't about to say anything that might get her in trouble with her master.

He studied her visually, and—in addition to the gaunt look, the shaved head, and the social security number tattooed across her forehead—he couldn't help but notice her rough hands and swollen raw feet. Though he hadn't met Ginger Bigelow, he had heard quite a bit about her, and he had seen pictures of her. She didn't resemble the thirty- something-year-old woman he had seen in pictures with the late Hiram Bigelow.

"I understand that you were Mr. Hiram Bigelow's wife. Is that true?" Doc asked.

She looked over at her Arab master, who nodded for her to go ahead and speak. "I was until he died, and I moved over here and met Abdul."

"What do you mean by that?" Doc asked. "Do you like where you're living and what you're doing?"

She again looked over at her Arab master and whined, "I can't go back."

"Why can't you go back, Mrs. Bigelow? Is it because of what happened to your husband, your stepdaughter, and Dr. Lowell? It's my understanding," Doc said, though he had no idea there was anything to it, "that you had something to do with their deaths. Are you afraid to go back and face the charges? Exactly why do you choose to stay? If you want to go back, maybe we can make arrangements through Muhammed to purchase you from Abdul and let you go back to the United States and stand trial."

When he said that, she screamed and covered her face. "No! No! I can't do that. Don't you see how I look?"

"What do you mean?" Doc asked. "Your hair will grow out, you can have the tattoo removed, your hands and feet will heal, and whatever happened between you and the men over here can soon be forgotten. Of course, you will have to stand trial for Mr. Hiram Bigelow's untimely demise and maybe for what happened to your stepdaughter, Lady Dee Bigelow Langford, and the young Dr. Lowell on their trip to the Amazon."

She panicked and screamed, "I didn't have anything to do with what happened to that bitch, Lady Dee, and Dr. Lowell, and I'm not going back."

"Why not, my dear?" Doc asked rather sarcastically. "If you didn't do anything wrong and Mr. Hiram died of natural causes, you have nothing to fear."

When he said that, he knew—or at least he thought he knew—that she had hastened her husband's demise. As to whether or not she had had anything to do with the deaths of her stepdaughter, Lady Dee, and Dr. Lowell, he didn't know.

"You mean to say, Ginger, that you are worried about what happened to your husband, as well as what happened to Mr. Bernard Swindle in the hotel in Chicago. I guess you made a mistake or two. You hired a not-so-sophisticated bunch of people to get rid of Swindle, and you didn't handle very deftly getting rid of your husband. Of course, I'm sure they are going to ask you about Lady Dee and Dr. Lowell. Now just make up your mind, because I'm getting ready to leave and you can either stay here or maybe go back with me to the States."

She broke down and started crying. With tears running down her face, she screamed, "What makes you think I killed that bastard, Bernie Swindle?"

"I didn't say you killed Mr. Swindle. All I said was that you hired Marta Roho and her group to kill Bernie Swindle." Doc deliberately didn't let her know whether or not Roho had been successful in trying to eliminate Swindle.

Abdul shouted at her in Arabic, and she immediately stiffened and stopped crying.

Doc asked Muhammed what Abdul said.

"In so many words he told her to shut up and act like a good wife, or he would give her fifty or a hundred lashes."

This made Doc cringe and think, *My goodness, do people really behave this way? Why did I ever let myself get involved?*

When Doc recovered sufficiently, he asked Ginger Bigelow if she had made up her mind.

She placed her burka back on her head and whined, "I can't go back, and if I obey Abdul, he will treat me a lot better than they will in prison for getting rid of that old husband of mine and Bernie Swindle."

Doc thought for the longest before trying to answer her. *Does she really think that being in a woman's prison in the United States would be worse than living in slavery married to Abdul?*

Muhammed turned to Doc and said, "Mr. Gibbs, what do you propose to do now that you know the option she has chosen?"

Doc hesitated before answering Muhammed. "I guess we'll let her have her way. Will you tell Abdul to try to take good care of his new wife?"

Muhammed told Abdul what Doc said, and he responded by saying something in Arabic that was interpreted by Muhammed to mean yes. He was going to take care of this good wife of his, and he would treat her like his other wives.

When Muhammed gave Abdul's response to Doc, he tensed up, regurgitated bile into his throat, and started to shake. "His other wives? My goodness."

Muhammed gave him a sarcastic smile and said, "Yes, Mr. Gibbs. He has one in Morocco, one in Saudi Arabia, and one with his brother in Afghanistan. He only sees them when he makes his occasional visit back home."

"Home? Where's home?" Doc forcefully asked.

"Oh, in the drug trade he travels between Morocco, Libya, Afghanistan, and Spain."

This was appalling to Doc, and he had no response other than to nod his head.

Chapter 40

Now that Roho and her crew had been annihilated, there was only one more question Doc wanted to get answered before he tried to make it back home. That was: what did Roho have in the ring on her finger when she scratched Swindle?

One of the French legionnaires told him that Marta Roho had a significant amount of sea snake venom on her person when they picked her up in Paris.

Doc asked, "How do you know?"

The older of the two Legionnaires said, "Because she told us. She was a big talker after being submerged in a well a few times. The other woman gave your burly black friend something called Flexoril in an effort to paralyze him or cause him to have enough muscle spasms to make him very sick and detain you until she could find the Roho woman."

Doc thought, *Dang, Swindle was very lucky, because some sea snakes are very poisonous. The Flexoril the girl gave Eldridge was nothing but a muscle relaxant. Of course, if you give them enough it will cause them to develop all sorts of symptoms, up to and including muscle spasms and the mental changes similar to what Eldridge experienced.*

Doc then told the Legionnaires that since they had shot up his car with a rocket, he was going to have to find some way to get back to where Sancho and Ramon had left their car.

Doc showed them his bleeding ankle with the brace on it and told them in no uncertain terms, "I'll do well to walk to the bottom of the hill, much less several miles."

The smaller of the two Germans replied, "Blackie big boy. He can carry you."

When he said that, Eldridge's neck veins started to swell, and he looked as if he was about to explode.

Doc cautioned him. "Eldridge, pay no attention to these people. You remember what I told you earlier about this game?"

Eldridge remembered Doc telling him that they were in the wrong place at the wrong time and in the wrong game, and as soon as they got out of it and back home, he felt they both should retire and do something else.

Doc was quick to say, "Men, you are very lucky. My friend Eldridge doesn't like being called blackie or boy. You should remember that in the future when you run into another black person, because they might not be as well disciplined as my dear friend here is."

The two Germans attempted to apologize. However, it was readily apparent that they didn't mean it.

Doc tried to overlook them and changed the subject. "Son, it looks like we need to be leaving here. What do you say, Eldridge?"

"If you say so, Mr. Gibbs."

"Well, Eldridge, I do say so. Now what do our two friends, Sancho and Ramon, have in mind as to how we can get back to their car in one piece?"

Sancho didn't trust the Germans, and he called Doc over, away from the crowd, and in a low voice said, "We've got the extra firepower, and we've got the grenades and plenty of explosives along with the automatic rifles. Unless these imbeciles are foolish enough to try and cause us any delay, we'll have no problems. Mr. Gibbs, I think you are absolutely right. We need to be leaving immediately, because someone is bound to have heard the noise, and Muhammed and those two worthless Germans can get a ride out of here on the helicopter when it makes its next regular drug run."

Doc found Muhammed back-talking to the Arabs and asked if he could arrange for them to rent a donkey or a cart.

"I'm a little behind schedule, so I need to be on my way as soon as possible. However, with my bad ankle I won't be able to make it up and down these steep hills. I figure I can ride a donkey, if they have one available."

After a few minutes of negotiating, it was agreed that one of the Arabs would take Doc out on his donkey.

Abdul again thanked him for the wife.

Doc didn't want to answer him, because he knew it was wrong and he regretted it, but he said begrudgingly, "The pleasure's all mine. I hope she ends up being your favorite wife."

With that, Doc bid them farewell, got on the donkey, and left with Eldridge, Sancho, Ramon, and the Arab who owned the donkey, hoping that Muhammed and the Germans would not do anything to try and stop them and they wouldn't run into the police.

Chapter 41

ALL THE WAY BACK TO where they had left Sancho and Ramon's car, they nervously carried on a nonsensical conversation. It was readily apparent that Doc and Eldridge wanted to forget about their experience at the Arab's domicile, so they started to talk about food.

"Eldridge, I'm about as hungry as you were when you said you could eat a whole hog. I sure would like to have some good food. You know the French are noted for their food, and it is good. The only trouble is that I can't read French, and some of these people won't wait on you unless you can speak French. That's how I ended up trying to eat the pasta and black truffles. Now, what would you really like to have if we had our choice of food right now?"

"Mr. Gibbs, to be honest with you I'd like to have some old-fashioned crackling bread, turnip greens cooked in a ham hock, black-eyed peas, and potlikker."

Doc smiled and said, "Dang, Eldridge, you're a man after my own heart. What part of the South are you from originally?"

Eldridge looked around to see if Sancho and Ramon were listening before answering. "I don't know how you knew, but I'm from Georgia."

"Serendipity, Eldridge, plus the way you act."

"That's a fine place. If I were you, when we get back and you get your hands on that alligator, if you know what I mean, I'd head back home and raise a few peaches or peanuts. Now if you get into the peanut business, I hope you'll do better than one of our former presidents, who was a so-called peanut farmer. Hard work will allow you to live a long, prosperous, and healthy life. Now, when it comes to food, I'd like to have a bunch of scrambled eggs, ham, some good buttermilk biscuits, and some old-fashioned hominy grits. What about you, lads?" Doc asked Sancho and Ramon.

"Oh, we'd like to have a good roasted pig for one thing," Sancho said.

Doc asked, "Where are you lads from originally?"

Ramon answered tentatively, afraid he might be breaking some of the rules. "We're from all over."

"Good," Doc commented. "You know, I've never eaten a roasted pig, but I understand it's a pretty common practice, particularly around Christmastime in parts of Cuba and different places."

When he said that, Sancho's eyes got big, and he tersely replied, "I didn't say we were from Cuba."

"I didn't say you were. That's just one of the many places I know of where they love to eat roasted suckling pigs, particularly around Christmastime. At least, that's what I understand. Of course, I don't really know, so let's drop the subject. How would y'all like to have some corn on the cob, slumgullion, and maybe punch pie? Y'all ever heard of punch pie? That's where you take an old apple pie off the rack at the supermarket and, after it's been baked, punch a hole in the crust and add a little rum or brandy to it. My goodness, I could add brother Eldridge's crackling bread, collard greens cooked in a ham hock with some potlikker, and black-eyed peas to the mix and be full for the rest of the day. But I guess that's not gonna happen until we get home. My, how I love 'white-trash cooking,' as the Yankees call it. Have you ever eaten skillet cornbread soaked in buttermilk and onions?"

When they finally reached the car, Sancho and Ramon had left. Doc thanked the Arab who had led the donkey and gave him a generous tip, and they got in the car and headed for Biarritz.

While en route, Doc asked Sancho what he planned to do when they got there and if he thought they should ditch the car before they got to town.

Sancho, who was driving, turned and smiled. "Don't worry, Mr. Gibbs, me and Ramon will take care of everything. I sure hope those boys that were making out on the beach don't get too upset when they find out what we've done to it."

Eldridge growled in his deep baritone voice, "What do you plan to do to it?"

"Oh," Ramon answered. "We'll have to destroy it. We can't afford to leave any fingerprints or anything behind. But I'm sure that if they have good government jobs, they can buy another one."

Doc didn't like the idea of destroying other people's property, but after what they had been through, almost anything they came up with as far as he was concerned wasn't as bad as what he had done. "Well, I'll leave that up to you young men. I think Eldridge and I will wander around town when we get there and maybe go to the beach. Of course, I hope Eldridge won't pick up another woman like the one from Lyon that gave him the Flexoril."

"Oh, Mr. Gibbs," Eldridge moaned, "aren't you ever gonna let me live that down? I'll never make that mistake again."

"I know you won't, son. You're a quick learner, and I imagine that you're going to do what we discussed a while back."

"What's that, Mr. Gibbs?" Eldridge looked puzzled.

"Go into early retirement. I'm worn out, and I don't have another job in me, so I'm going back to jail."

When Doc said that, both Ramon and Sancho gave him a blank stare. Surprised, Eldridge asked, "What are you in jail for?"

"It's a long story, son; it's a long story. Remember, that's where I was before I came to Chicago. I'm just out on bail, and I've gotta go back and face the charges against me and maybe serve a term. Of course, that's not too bad, all things considered, since the sheriff and I play poker."

"Play poker?" Sancho asked.

"Yeah, strip poker."

Eldridge was somewhat shocked by his remark and replied, "Why would you play strip poker with the sheriff?"

"Yeah," Sancho said.

"Well, to tell you the truth, this is a lady sheriff. She's thirty-five or -six years old and built like a brick outhouse, as us country folks say."

"What does that mean, Mr. Gibbs?" Ramon asked.

"Aw, Ramon, it means that she is built like a beauty queen, I guess you could say."

"What if you lose?" Sancho asked.

"Huh, that could be a problem, but I don't think I'm gonna lose. I never have so far. When I left the poor sheriff, after I made bail, she was naked as a jaybird before I gave her some clothes back to wear until we could finish the game."

Eldridge interrupted, “Can’t you play the game without being in jail?”

“Yeah, I sure can, but I don’t know how long I’m gonna be in there. It just depends on how things work out.”

“What are you in there for?” Ramon asked. “You kill someone again?”

“No, it’s worse than that. There’s this woman who’s accusing me of taking unfair advantage of her forty-six-year-old daughter—which, in my case, if you no doubt noticed how old and worn out I am, is a very remote possibility. If not, it’s an improbability.”

The whole time this was going on, Doc was trying to forget all that had happened since he had left the Hooker County Jail with Boobs to go see Swindle. It was working to some extent, because by spinning his partially true story he was becoming more relaxed and feeling almost human again.

When they reached the outskirts of Biarritz, they got out of the car, and Sancho and Ramon instructed Doc and Eldridge to walk on in to town while they doused the car with gasoline they were siphoning from the tank to set it on fire.

Chapter 42

Doc stretched on a rotten beach chair with his fez over his face in an effort to go to sleep. It had been almost forty-eight hours since he had actually had even a short nap, but sleep would not come. He kept thinking about where he had been and what he had done. The mere thought of it was awful. To start with, why had he gone to Chicago to help Swindle? It was like Mertis had said. There were more good doctors in Chicago than there were in the whole state where he lived. That was bad enough, but when he got there and found that Swindle had not been poisoned to the extent that it was life threatening, why hadn't he left? Why had he tried to find out who the girl from Ipanema was who had visited Swindle? Why had he called Turner and gotten mixed up with the crowd who helped him capture the so-called girl from Ipanema, Marta Roho? The whole thing was more than he could bear.

He figured the only thing he had tried to do right was to follow Muhammed to France to make sure that he didn't kill Roho and the person who turned out to be Ginger Bigelow, who had hired Roho's group to kill Swindle. He had even failed at that. He and his friend Eldridge had left a trail of mayhem and murder wherever they had been. The girl from Lyon had been killed, along with the group that came to rescue her. Roho had run down the hill from the cottage, only to be killed by her friends. He had personally killed two or three people. How could he have done it? He didn't know. A doctor was supposed to do everything possible to improve the quality of a person's life and help him live as long as possible. To top it off, he had left Ginger Bigelow behind with her Arab master.

He flounced around a while longer, only to get out of the lounge chair and go look for Eldridge. He had to do something. He couldn't live with himself, thinking that he had been a passive participant in allowing Ginger Bigelow, who was without a doubt a murderer, to be left behind in slavery to Abdul.

Doc walked the beach, and when he didn't find Eldridge he went to the bathhouse, where he thought Eldridge had changed into his thong, and found him on the floor naked with two French women working him over.

He removed his fez and passively said, "Ladies, if you are about through with my friend Eldridge, would you mind letting him go? We have something we need to do. It's of the utmost importance that we start immediately."

The two French women stopped giving Eldridge a trip around the world and turned and smiled at him. They said something in French to the effect that they would be through momentarily. With that, he turned and left the bathhouse until they finished what they were doing.

When the women left, Doc made sure that they hadn't rolled the prostrate Eldridge.

Eldridge had a hard time putting his clothes on. He located his wallet, his papers, and his money and, after looking around for a while, found the .44 Magnum pistol stuffed under the floor of the bathhouse.

Doc cleared his throat and said, "Eldridge, we've got to go back and see Muhammed and the Arabs."

"Why, Mr. Gibbs?"

"It's very simple. We have participated in allowing someone to be sold or given away. You should be more aware of it than I am, since your ancestors were brought over from Africa against their will and sold into slavery."

This struck a cord with Eldridge, and he gave Doc a startled look before responding. "Mr. Gibbs, she said she wanted to stay, didn't she?"

"That's what she said, all right, Eldridge. She sure did. She said she wanted to stay, but one has to ask why she said she wanted to stay. Would it have been similar to what your great-great-grandmother would have said when she was in the slave quarters and someone walked in out of the blue and asked her if she wanted to go with them or stay behind with the master? I wonder what she would have said. I think I know. She would have said she wanted to stay. Now think about it, Eldridge, you know I'm right."

Eldridge instinctively knew that Doc was right and that, even though she was a murderer and would have to stand trial for at least one and maybe two murders if she returned to the States, she should have the right to choose. She should be free to make the choice. With that, he zipped up his trousers, searched through his jacket again to make sure that nothing was missing, and accompanied Doc outside.

Doc picked up his valise, looked up at Eldridge, and said, "I've given this a lot of thought. I'm an old man with a bum leg, and my time's about up. If I have to go now, I want to know that I've tried to do right by this young woman. There's no way we can bring back the others. They're gone of their own choosing. It's bad enough to have to kill 'em, but like you said, it was either us or them. Now you don't have to go."

Eldridge looked down at him and bellowed out in his deep baritone voice, "The hell I don't. I ain't in no slavery business, plus I gotta make sure you get back all right, so I can get my hands on that tan alligator briefcase we left in the bank in New Orleans."

When he said that, Doc reached down and removed his right shoe, lifted up the inner sole, and handed him a slip of paper with the number and key to the safe deposit box that contained the money. "No, son, you can leave right now. The money's yours. I made a promise, and I'm gonna keep it. Now you don't have to go, but I'm going."

Eldridge responded in a mournful tone, "Aw hell, Mr. Gibbs, stick that back in your shoe. I'm going with you, since you put it that way. You damn well know I don't believe in slavery."

With that, they left to go find a cab.

Chapter 43

THEY FOUND A MAN WHO was willing to drive them to the Arabs' camp. The driver spoke some English, thus making it impossible for them to discuss their plans, other than mention they were going to try to negotiate a trade.

The driver was from Eritrea and cared little about what they were actually up to, as long as he got his money. They negotiated a price, paid, and left.

After traveling over rough, hilly terrain, they arrived at the compound where the Arabs were camped. Rather than stopping and walking the last several hundred yards, Doc instructed the driver to drive on up to the stone cottage.

The poor man, not knowing what he was getting into, did as they suggested. Before they got out of the car, they told him they wouldn't be there over an hour, if all went well with the transaction.

They got out and walked up to where two of the Arabs were sitting around an open fire, cooking a hare. Not being able to speak Arabic, Doc asked for Muhammed.

One of the young Arabs, who could speak a little English, told them that Muhammed had left on the helicopter for Marseille with the two Germans.

Doc then asked where Abdul was. Before he could get an answer, Abdul came out of the cottage with a rather sarcastic smile on his face and welcomed them back.

Doc told the young man to tell Abdul that he and his friend had returned to negotiate with him for the return of the woman Muhammed had given him.

Abdul gave them an angry look and finally said, through the young man who was acting as the interpreter, "What do they want to talk to me about my wife for?"

Doc was so frightened that his insides were shaking, but he managed to forcefully reply, again through the interpreter. "I want to negotiate with you the purchase of the woman."

When the young man told Abdul what Doc had said, he laughed and responded, "What can an old man like you do with a young wife like her?"

The young man told Doc what he said, and he quickly responded, "I can, if nothing else, get her to keep me warm on cold nights and cook my meals. Now what will you take for the woman?"

Abdul said to the interpreter, "I don't want to give up the woman. She's very clean, has not been used very much. Two of my wives stink."

"What do you mean, stink?" Doc asked as firmly as he could, still wearing the voice amplification device.

"Pee through wrong place and stink!" Abdul answered through the interpreter.

"Oh, how old were they when you married them and they had their first child?"

"Eleven years old and cost me a camel for one and eight goats for another one."

Both Doc and Eldridge cringed when they heard this. It was obvious to Doc that they had both been so young when they had their first child that they had perforated the wall between the vagina and bladder, and that was the reason for them smelling.

Doc's first thought was, *My goodness, I hope this is not a common practice. I do understand, though, that it's not uncommon. Sooner or later someone's going to have to put a stop to it.*

Doc was now not only scared, he was angry at the thought of the two young girls' fathers selling them for a camel and eight goats. The very idea was reprehensible to him. He knew that if they didn't have some sort of surgery done, they would no doubt be shunned by everyone except maybe a member of their family.

He looked over at Eldridge and said, "Eldridge, it's imperative that we talk to Ginger Bigelow and make sure she is free to choose her future."

Eldridge asked, "What if she's so scared she'll say she wants to stay?"

"I don't know. I think if she understands exactly what's going on, and I'm sure she does, that she will make one or the other options—that is, if Abdul will relinquish her for a price."

"Relinquish her?" Eldridge questioned.

"Yes, if he will sell her to us."

With that, Doc turned back to Abdul and said, "I'm going to make you an offer you can't resist. You can always find another woman and maybe better without a tattoo on her head that is a lot younger. This one's a little old, and at best you can only have one or two children with her. Now let's go inside and talk."

When he said that, Abdul motioned for them to follow him into the cottage, where they took a seat on the dirt floor.

Chapter 44

DOC AND ELDRIDGE SAT FACING Abdul and the young man who could speak English, and Doc started to haggle with Abdul about Ginger Bigelow.

Doc figured it would cost roughly seven thousand dollars for the surgery to repair the bladder-vaginal fistula his two other brides had and offered him fifteen thousand dollars. Normally he would have offered him more, but he knew that they were in the opium trade and that money wasn't particularly a problem. It was just a matter of pride for Abdul.

Abdul steadfastly refused, and Doc countered. "Do you care very much about your two wives who stink?"

Abdul responded, "Had to send them back home. Lost a camel and eight goats."

"What would you think," Doc replied, "if they could get the fistula repaired between their ruptured bladder and vagina? Would you want them back?"

Abdul thought for the longest time before answering as usual through the interpreter, "I'm not sure I understand you."

Doc took his finger and drew in the dirt the location of the bladder and the vagina and told him what the problem was. "If this problem can be repaired, which it can, they will be as good as new, and these two wives of yours will be at least twenty years younger than the woman you got from Muhammed."

Abdul didn't seem to comprehend.

Doc tried again. He took his finger and showed him that the bladder was the place that collected the urine and that the fistula or rupture into the wrong place was what was causing the odor.

Abdul still didn't understand.

Doc then said, "What if we could cure the stink and make them like new? What would you say?"

"Oh, maybe so. Then I would have both women, and maybe I could get their daddies to give back the camel and goats if I take them."

Eldridge was appalled at the conversation. From the tone of Doc's voice, he knew that Doc was also, but he kept his mouth shut.

Doc then asked, "What about sixteen thousand dollars or the equivalent in euros?"

Abdul again answered, "I'll take twenty thousand dollars for the used woman."

They haggled a little longer, and Doc finally raised his voice. "Abdul, I've got to go shortly. Now let's close this deal. I'll split the difference with you—seventeen and a half thousand, and I'll get the old woman. You'll have enough money, along with what you're going to make from the opium, to do anything in the world you want to. There are a lot of women out there—plenty of French, Spanish, and Muslim women all over Africa and the Middle East. You name it. Now what do you want? I need the old woman. I do not have a woman." This was a lie, but he told it.

Abdul said through the interpreter, "Make it twenty, and you take the woman and leave in peace."

Doc turned to Eldridge and asked if he had twenty thousand to spare.

Eldridge counted out the money, placed it on the dirt floor in front of Abdul, and the deal was made. Now all he needed to do was see if he could get Ginger Bigelow and leave this place.

While Abdul was getting Ginger ready to go, Doc and Eldridge stepped outside. He asked Eldridge if he knew where Sancho and Ramon had placed all the explosives.

Eldridge looked at him and asked, "Why?"

"Eldridge, I don't trust these people, and you know I have Sancho's phone he left in my valise, so I can detonate them as soon as we leave, if necessary, and hopefully escape with our skins. Anyway, we owe it to this fine young man from Eritrea to make sure he gets back to Biarritz safely and collects his fee."

"Oh, okay. You still got the pistols and sniper rifle?"

"Yes, Eldridge. Why do you think I brought the valise? I've also got some of the plastic explosives, along with the detonation devices and the phone. When we get Ms. Bigelow, we'll be on our way."

"Whatta you gonna do with the Bigelow woman?"

"We have freed her to see if she wants to be free. That's the best we can do. She can choose to do whatever she wants."

"I'm not sure I follow you, Mr. Gibbs."

"Quite simply, she can stay here and work in France and try to avoid prosecution in the United States, or she can return home and stand trial for murder. I believe she's at least responsible for her husband's early death. I don't know about the deaths of her stepdaughter and Dr. Lowell. Those could have been the old man's doing. He was an evil old man who had some dealings with a company in Brazil, so I've been told."

"You mean to say her husband would kill his own daughter."

"Oh yeah, he's a trial lawyer, you know."

Chapter 45

Eldridge and Doc were joined shortly by Abdul and Ginger Bigelow. Doc thanked Abdul and said, "With your permission, we will leave. Maybe sometime in the future we can make another deal." This was a lie. As far as Doc and Eldridge were concerned, all they wanted to do was get out of there and never see them again.

Eldridge was still upset about the Germans who were members of the French Foreign Legion getting away. After all, they had called him a "smoke" and a "boy" and no telling what else behind his back. He got in the backseat with a foul-smelling Ginger Bigelow, and Doc, carrying his valise, got in the front.

The young Eritrean turned his car around and started back down the side of the rather steep hill. About halfway down, Doc took out one of the plastic explosives, placed a detonator device in it, set it by the side of the road, and got out the phone.

This frightened the driver. He felt that he was into something illegal. Doc assured him that he wasn't, that he was totally innocent, and that what they were doing was just making sure that they were not being followed by a bunch of stray bandits. The driver didn't believe him, but he nodded yes.

Doc then turned to Ginger and said, "You are free to choose."

When he said that, she started crying. "I can never be free. Can't you see me?"

"Oh, yes. Your hair will grow out in time, and you can wear a band around your forehead to cover up the tattoo until you can earn enough money to have it removed. Of course, there are other options. One would be to go back to the States and stand trial. Now that you're free, what do you choose to do? Now if you want to, I can get this young man to stop the car and let you out, and you can go back up to Abdul. Now you have these three choices. Which one are you going to make?"

She continued to sob, drenching her face with tears. Finally, before the trip was completed, she chose to stay in France and work.

Doc looked at Eldridge and said, "Do you think we can buy her a wig, some clothes, and a headband so she can look for gainful employment? I rather doubt that she wants to go back to where she was living in the south of France, since she no longer has any money."

The driver was taking all this in but keeping his mouth shut. Doc then turned to him and asked if he knew where a young woman, who had been sold into bondage, could find a job in the south of France.

He told him that he knew a man who ran a restaurant, who was looking for a dishwasher. Would she clean up?

Doc then turned to Ginger and sarcastically said, "Well, that'll be a start if you choose to stay."

She didn't hesitate. She said she would gladly take the job as a dishwasher, rather than returning to the States. All the time she was thinking about how she could get away and get back to the old man she had been living with in Monaco. The only question in her mind was if he would have her after he found out what had happened to her. Being the skilled liar that she had always been, she assumed that she could tell him that she had been kidnapped, and he would no doubt believe her, since he was a man in his late sixties like her late husband.

Doc asked Eldridge what he thought about this. Eldridge agreed, and when they reached Biarritz he instructed the driver to take her by a modest lady's clothing store. Several streets off the main boulevard, he stopped the car in front of a rather nondescript women's ready-to-wear boutique. They purchased her a fairly decent dress and a pair of Birkenstock sandals for her swollen feet. After purchasing a wig and a headband at another establishment, they let her out of the car at a restaurant that needed a dishwasher, and Doc wished her the best of luck.

Doc wasn't sure what she was up to but figured she was up to some of her usual tricks and would no doubt try to make connections with someone she knew in France before taking the job as a dishwasher.

Chapter 46

NOW THAT GINGER HAD GOTTEN out of the car, Doc asked the Eritrean what he would charge to drive them to Paris. He quoted them a price, and they accepted.

Since neither Doc nor Eldridge had eaten in quite some time, they asked him where they could purchase a good meal before they left. He quickly obliged and took them to his cousin's shop.

Eldridge had been keeping his eye on the Eritrean ever since they had left Ginger to make sure he didn't report them. While they were waiting on their meal, Eldridge stayed within an arm's length of him the entire time.

Suddenly, Doc decided that since they had the valise with all the guns, hand grenades, and plastic explosives in it, they needed to catch a freighter that was headed for New Orleans. When they got back in the car, Doc informed the driver to take them to the closest commercial dock. He had decided against going to Paris.

They were in luck. There was a ship in the local port loaded with stolen Mercedes automobiles headed to the Port of New Orleans. Doc and Eldridge bribed the captain to let them go once they had him convinced they were not the law.

Before they left, they paid the Eritrean for the trip to Paris that they didn't take.

This made him smile, and as they left to board the ship, he said, "Thank you. I hope the rest of your trip goes well."

"Me too," Doc replied. "I'm sure you can attest to the fact that there was nothing out of the ordinary that happened during the time we were with you, other than the fact that we freed a poor, dirty woman who had been sold into slavery."

The Eritrean nodded and waved as they boarded the ship.

Chapter 47

Doc and Eldridge stayed to themselves on the trip over while the ship carrying the stolen German Mercedes bounced around and slowly made its way to New Orleans. Normally they would have been worried, but there was a mixed crew from all over the world, and they were never more than an arm's length from their weapons.

The captain of the freighter asked them several times who they were running from, and Doc told him that they were getting out of France and headed back home and that they, like them, had some illegal goods to deliver. The captain tried to see if they were talking about diamonds or rubies or things of that nature, but Doc was quick to tell him that he was carrying a new kind of explosive, but not to worry; they were safe. This frightened the captain but, knowing he was guilty of exporting stolen cars, said nothing.

When they arrived in New Orleans, they thanked the captain for the long bumpy ride and went immediately to the Café Du Monde, ordered a cup of the café's famous chicory coffee, and decadently dunked all the beignets they could eat into the elixir.

When they finished eating, Doc stood, rubbed his belly gently, and said, "Thank the Lord I'm full again. Eldridge, what do you say we go shower and shave and get your money?"

Once they had gotten rid of the valise and taken a shower and shaved, they went to Brooks Brothers, bought some light summer clothes, and proceeded to the bank for the money.

When they left the bank, Doc shook Eldridge's hand and said, "That's it for me. I'm going back to jail. What are you going to do, Eldridge?"

Eldridge had a quick reply. "Find me a woman, Mr. Gibbs, and go home to Georgia and grow peanuts."

Doc pulled his old hat with the burned-out crown out of his coat pocket and bade him farewell.

Eldridge said, "One more thing before you leave. How did you come up with the name 'the girl from Ipanema'? It couldn't have been Roho or any of the women we ran into."

"Eldridge, I wish you hadn't asked, but here's what happened."

Chapter 48

ELDRIDGE PULLED ON HIS LOWER lip, looked down at Dr. Suggs, and asked, "One more question before I go, Mr. Gibbs."

"What's that, son?"

"Who was the girl from Ipanema?"

"I was so busy following all the people involved in this case and forgot about her till we were talking to Ginger Bigelow. That's when I realized there was no girl from Ipanema."

"How so?" Eldridge asked.

"Eldridge, when Roho mounted Swindle, she had her tape recorder playing 'The Girl from Ipanema.' I didn't know then, and I don't know now, if Ginger Bigelow wasn't sending a death message to Swindle."

"How so, Mr. Gibbs?"

"Ginger was a scorned woman, whereas Roho was just a stupid person Carlos wanted to get rid of so he could have the three Peace Corps girls to himself if she failed."

"So it couldn't have been her."

"The nun from Lyon who could play more tricks on you than a monkey could on a grapevine was never in the picture, except to find out what we knew about where Roho was and to slow us down by giving you the Flexoril. You know she was kinda like some female spiders. They kill the male after they breed them."

"Oh, Mr. Gibbs, why did you bring that up?"

"To remind you not to have sex with someone you don't know very well. Now that leaves the scorned woman, Ginger Bigelow."

"Why did Ginger Bigelow hate him so much?"

"They had been having this tempestuous affair ever since Swindle went to work at the Bigelow firm, and they even went so far as to do it in the old man's bed on Wednesday nights when he played poker, until he came home early one night and caught them nude, sharing a joint, and playing her favorite song, 'The Girl from Ipanema.' They panicked, set the bed on fire, and Swindle jumped out the window naked with old man Bigelow shooting at him. That's why some people who know about it called Swindle 'Smokey the Bare.' Ginger tried to rekindle their affair, but he was too scared of Bigelow to run the risk of getting caught again or ending up maybe having to marry her. He liked more than one woman."

"Oh," Eldridge replied.

"I'm not sure, Eldridge, but she is one more scorned woman. Anyway, we accomplished most of what we set out to do and freed a slave. So let's try to forget about the girl from Ipanema and move on."

"I guess so, Mr. Gibbs," Eldridge agreed as he got in a cab to take him to the airport.